Captcha This!

Also by J. W. Wood

POETRY

Swingtime (Southside Press, 1991)
The Theory of Everything (Happenstance Press, 2006)
Inextinguishable (The Knucker Press, 2008)
The Anvil's Prayer (Ward/Wood Publishing, 2013)
The Emigrant's Farewell (The High Window, 2016)
Building a Kingdom: New and Selected Poems, 1989–2019 (The High Window, 2019)

FICTION (as Craig Sterling)
Stealing Fire (Leamington Books, 2011)

Captcha This!

J. W. Wood

an editions

AN Editions
aneditions.co.uk | editors@aneditions.com

British Library Cataloguing in Publication Data
A catalogue record for this book is available from the British Library

ISBN 978-1-7384023-3-5

In memory of Stephen S. Thompson, writer and friend, 1966–2022.

"singing sweet songs
with melodies pure and true…"
—**Bob Marley,** *Three Little Birds*

CONTENTS

SHOW PONIES 1

FOR ONE NIGHT ONLY 17

FLARE-UP! 24

CRUNCH TIME FOR THE PHEASANT 34

A RIVETING TALE 46

BY ANY OTHER NAME 54

MY GRANDMOTHER'S RUSSIAN DOLL 79

ANTI-SOCIAL 92

RESIGNATION 98

YOU LOOK LIKE YOU'RE WRITING A NOVEL 109

Acknowledgements 113

Show Ponies

John Iwelumu rested a hand on the withers of his four-year-old thoroughbred, Lightning, who snorted and shook his mane. John whispered in his ear to calm him.

This was the year. The year he'd take the podium at the Palladian Horse Trials – the world's biggest equestrian event. A million pounds prize money, a crowd of 60,000, worldwide media. Forget everything he'd done as an entrepreneur, family man or role model for youth – in a few weeks, he would bust open a world of class, money and privilege for everyone to enjoy.

Iwelumu looked around his stable block, those walls of honeyed Cotswold stone. Not bad for a pikny bwai from Tottenham Hale. But Iwelumu wanted more: and he'd get it, no matter what it took.

§

"Who the devil are you?"

Major Justin Carr did not suffer fools – and never missed the chance to tell them what they were. After thirty years serving Queen and Country, the administration of an equestrian event might seem a comedown. But society required he take some occupation to supplement his pension, especially since said annuity barely covered Caroline's flower bill.

"I'm sorry. I thought this was the interview room."

"It is."

"Oh right. Hi – I'm Nabila."

Major Carr fingered his cufflinks and inspected the interviewee. She looked like a metropolitan meddler who'd lived in some dreadful box in Acton before decamping to Gloucestershire.

"Well? Come in." Carr's eyebrows relaxed a little. "Coffee or tea?"

"Oh – no thanks. I don't drink caffeine," the woman said.

Definitely metropolitan. He shook hands, noting the woman's

dark brown hair cascading onto her turquoise *shalwar kameez*. Different from the local women, who dressed in quilted jackets, tweed skirts, that sort of thing.

Carr ran a tired hand through what was left of his hair. He was bally useless at interviewing. The Palladian board always solicited his opinion – then did whatever they wanted. Their latest wheeze was the hire of a "Diversity Co-ordinator". Stuff and nonsense. He'd never had such things in the forces, and didn't need one now. No one was stopping anyone from attending, competing in or watching the Palladians.

"So, er, tell me. What makes you want to work with horses?"

"Well, it's not about horses *per se*. I'm more passionate about diversity."

"I see."

Carr gazed out the window, trying not to give his thoughts away. This time the board would have to compromise, not him. And he knew exactly how to get them to do it.

§

The next morning, grooms Annabella and Janet were on a break. They'd spent the morning transporting horseshit and wood shavings from the stables to a muck heap located at a discreet distance, then doing it again. And again.

"What you up to this weekend?" Janet asked, one eye on the chocolate biscuits on the tearoom table.

"Point-to-point with Charlie," chirruped Annabella, pulling her white-gold hair back into a loose bob and lighting a cigarette. "Then probably din-dins in some pub or other. You?"

"Not much."

For all that Janet envied Annabella's looks, she found her as dull as a dishcloth mouldering under a sink. The same parties, the same people. Her boyfriend, Charlie, even used the same phrases constantly: "finest chap in Christendom", "sound as a pound" and whatnot.

"Such a shame. It's the away-day on Monday. Plenty of frolics there! Anyway, I'm going to let you in on a secret…."

Janet groaned inwardly. Probably something about someone Annabella suspected of voting Labour.

"What is it?"

"Well," Annabella smiled, billowing smoke from her cigarette. "At the away-day, yours truly will be announced as our new Diversity Co-ordinator." She dropped her voice to a stage whisper. "Old Major Carr told the board to Foxtrot Oscar when they wanted a Diversity Co-ordinator, but had to give in. No more horse turds for me!"

Janet drained her tea and stood up, wafting Annabella's smoke away.

"Where are you going? I've just lit a cigarette!"

"I'm off to brush Cannonball. Major Carr says he wants to ride him today."

Annabella sneered.

"Let his girth out a hole or two, would you? If Carr's saddle slips it might frighten some life into the old bugger."

§

The away-day was a misnomer, since it took place on the Palladian estate. But at least it was a relief from shovelling shit – though perhaps shit of a different kind was about to be shovelled.

Major Carr ordered Annabella to be at his office at 0800 – thirty minutes before coffee in the grooms' quarters. Fiercely proud of the commission he had received from our Late Queen, Carr wore claret-coloured moleskin jeans and a checked shirt – standard issue casualwear for an ex-military man.

He turned from the window and fixed his hawk's eye on Annabella, who'd entered without knocking.

"Well?"

"Well what?"

Annabella wore a fine black cashmere rollneck and skinny blue jeans, one silver-bangled hand on her hip.

"Where's my diversity and inclusion plan?"

"Oh – er, may I sit down?"

Major Carr nodded to the chair where Nabila sat last Thursday.

"Now look here. Before this away-day whatsit kicks off, let's be clear."

Annabella sat down and leaned forward. She knew the old boy had a thing for her. Where's the harm in a little flirting?

"This diversity thing is bollocks. But we need to be seen to do it.

So when I announce your new role, use the right terms. You know, upreach or inreach or—"

"You mean the outreach programme I'm preparing, Justin?"

"That's Major Carr to you, young lady. Don't get saucy or you'll go over my knee."

"Promises, promises, Major Carr. Anyway, here's my idea. We get some inner-city types and give them mentoring."

"Mentoring?"

"You know: training as a groom. Mucking out. Being a jockey."

"A jockey? Ridiculous."

Annabella gazed out the window, wondering if there'd be snacks with coffee. She'd skipped breakfast, not wanting to plump up like poor Janet. Major Carr drew her back—

"Who in hell would mentor such lowlifes? I mean, who'll lead this?"

"Someone who wants to 'give something back' – you know, a do-gooder wanting to raise their social standing."

Major Carr touched the silver cigarette case on his desk – his father's – as he often did while thinking.

"There is someone you could speak to, I suppose."

"Who?"

"That Iwelumu fellow. You know the one: insurance broker on the telly. Owns an estate in Hampshire."

Annabella got up and walked towards the door, then spun round, twirling her hair.

"So I'm supposed to persuade someone I've never met to train thugs in riding and get them to foot the bill? Well: can't wait for my next payrise – Major Carr."

Carr straightened his regimental tie.

"Mr Iwelumu is our major sponsor through his company, Sand Dollar Insurance Services. We have invited him here today to discuss the topic of diversity. I'm sure you'll be able to persuade him, Miss Amphlett. That's all."

Major Carr admired Annabella's departing form. What a filly. But then, what was true of horses was true of women – the best-looking ones are more trouble than they're worth. Maybe I'm being sexist, he thought. But I'm too old to care now.

§

A few hours later, all Palladian staff – from Major Carr to the lowliest stable hand – crowded into the old grooms' quarters for the first session after lunch. They were slumping in carb coma after those heaped plates of smoked salmon wraps and rare roast beef sandwiches. The hall's beams, darkened by centuries of woodsmoke, groaned with the weight of garish motivational slogans: EVERY GUEST DELIGHTED; I+TEAM=US.

Major Carr squinted over half-moon spectacles at his laptop perched on an old lectern from the estate chapel.

"Right. What's next? Oh yes. Diversity and Inclusion. Our board have decided we need a Diversity and Inclusion policy. After an extensive process, we have appointed Annabella Amphlett to lead this vital initiative. So, without further fanfare – Bella, over to you!"

Janet fixed her eyes forward as Annabella's heels clacked to the lectern, noting bright pink paisley shoes with red soles and two-inch heels. Why Annabella? She was to inclusivity what Vlad the Impaler was to the Geneva Convention.

Janet mentally prepared herself for an onslaught of vacuous piffle.

"Thank you, Major Carr," beamed Annabella, strategically placed blonde strands falling over her china-blue eyes. "I am simply delighted to take on the DEI brief—"

"The what?" Carr queried.

"The DEI brief. Diversity, Equity and Inclusion. That's what they call it in London."

"I see. Well, carry on then, man – I mean woman."

"Thank you."

Annabella outlined her strategy with the sincerity of a Miss Universe contestant preaching about rain forests. For too long, she said, horse trials had been the province of a rich, white elite. But it was time for these antediluvian (bet she had to look that up, Janet thought) attitudes to change. For the Palladian Trials to move into the twenty-first century.

"And that's why we are introducing mentoring for inner-city youth who've experienced incarceration events," Annabella concluded, her announcement followed by a terse wither of applause.

"You mean prisoners? Lags? Bugger me, I don't remember agreeing to that," Carr expostulated.

"To help us in this task, I'm delighted to welcome Mr John Iwelumu, MBE, founder of Sand Dollar Insurance Services. A keen horseman, Mr Iwelumu has agreed to chair our DEI initiative. John?"

Being – to use the correct term – visibly different from everyone else, John Iwelumu couldn't have blinked without being noticed. Instead, he capitalised on his difference and strode towards the lectern. The audience recognised him from TV ads for pet insurance and began clapping.

"Thank you, thank you. This is the high point of my life. Of course, I've done well in business. And I cherish my family. But the chance to get involved in changing equestrianism. Well – that's beyond my dreams."

Iwelumu explained how his mother had brought him up on a different kind of estate – "one with concrete and villains, not fields and trees" – after his father died. How he'd worked his way up from teaboy to running one of Britain's biggest insurance companies. And how he'd done it all in the face of constant prejudice and bigotry.

"And now I want to give something back. That's why I'm sponsoring the first candidates for the Palladian DEI programme at my estate. Teaching troubled young people how – as the great R. S. Surtees said many years ago – the relationship between human and horse is the greatest ever known."

The hall swelled with applause. Even Major Carr looked impressed. Only Janet did not clap – and not because she didn't like Iwelumu. She just wondered if this nineteenth-century relic could ever adapt to the modern world.

§

DuWayne Anderson stood in the dock at Bermondsey Magistrates Court looking at a two to four stretch. He'd never wanted to push white – he just had to get out of the Ends. And football or peddling was the only way man knew. After he'd been let go by Leicester City's Academy at sixteen, there was just one way out – selling drugs.

He rubbed his wrist where his Rolex used to be, staring out the barred window of the prisoner transport that brought him to John

Iwelumu's estate. With lush veridian lawns stretching to the horizon, this place was beyond his imagination. He'd said yes to this racket because his choices were three more years inside or four picking up litter with a tag on his leg. Next to that, two years riding horses was a dream.

The transport pulled up and a bloke in three-quarter-length white trousers, tweed jacket and riding boots approached. He had a shovel in one hand and a massive Roller on his wrist. Man must have some peas.

DuWayne disembarked and the guy stretched out his hand.

"Welcome to Goldswater. I'm John Iwelumu."

"Right, blud? Safe." DuWayne reached out his fist to bump Iwelumu's fingertips. "Got any niyinyam, fam? Man starvin' after that trip, innit?"

DuWayne felt his legs fly out under him. Iwelumu dropped on him, grabbing his cornrows.

"Listen to me – fam. Drop the badman act, cos you just met someone badder than you. Get me?"

DuWayne stared up at Iwelumu's face, smelled the expensive cologne, clocked the sharp threads.

"I said you get me – fam?"

DuWayne nodded to indicate that he had, indeed, comprehended. Iwelumu stood up and dusted off his jodhpurs, made sure his timepiece was clean and straightened his collar.

"As I was saying. Your first task will be assisting hygiene maintenance in the stable block."

Iwelumu jerked a thumb behind him. DuWayne peered round his host to see the biggest pile of shit he had ever seen in his life. This time, Iwelumu's accent was more East End crim than landowning classes—

"That lot. To the gardens. By twelve. Otherwise it's back inside. Ya feel me – bro?"

Iwelumu handed DuWayne the shovel and stalked off towards his enormous Tudor mansion. DuWayne contemplated the pile of horseshit, then the wheelbarrow. An old man in turd-encrusted overalls came out of the stables and waved at DuWayne. Suddenly the idea of a three-year stretch looked more appealing....

§

Janet sat by herself in the tearoom with a mug and a chocolate biscuit, mired in reverie. Somehow she'd preferred old Annabella to new Annabella, a woman who raced around the stable block putting up posters and sending emails to staff about "awareness sessions" to discuss their "unconscious bias".

Major Carr popped his head round the door.

"Ah, Janet. There you are. Mind if I sit down?"

"Feel free, Major Carr."

"Thank you. This looks like the only place to get a break from posters and emails, what? If I get one more lecture about my historic crimes, I'll—"

"Well, society is changing, Major Carr."

Before Janet could say more, Annabella breezed in with a poster flapping behind her. Her new-found political awareness notwithstanding, Janet noticed Annabella still wore the Hermès scarf Charlie bought her in a moment of drunken sincerity.

"Hope you'll all be coming to the Palladian's Roots in Slavery exhibition next month," sing-songed Annabella. "Oh and Janet – Charlie's brother is doing a Vicars and Tarts party next weekend. Fancy it? We need to find you a boyfriend."

"I find such gatherings offend the rights of faith-based persons and sex workers," Janet replied, popping half a Hobnob in her mouth. "And your presumptions regarding my sexuality are an outrage. But I might make it – we'll see."

"I'll let you ladies carry on." Carr jolted upright from the table. "Someone's got to run the bloody show: the trials start in twelve weeks."

He strode out, causing Annabella's poster to flap violently where she'd stuck it to the tearoom wall. Annabella sat down and lit up.

"Why is he so cross? I'm just doing my job," she said through a cloud of smoke.

Janet took a long sip of tea. Who needed Vicars and Tarts parties when work offered such never-ending amusement?

§

DuWayne arose at five to execute his quotidian obligation regarding horseshit, forking it out of the stables and ferrying it to the muck heap. Mr Iwelumu said he had something different for him after lunch: just as well, cos man would rather be in the pen than do this shit (literally) for another two years.

After lunch, DuWayne met John Iwelumu by the stables dressed in full riding gear, holding Lightning by the reins.

"Look at this horse," said Iwelumu. "What do you see?"

"Horse, innit. White one."

"It's centuries of breeding. It's a bloodline that goes back before the Napoleonic Wars. A thoroughbred whose ancestors carried kings into battle. Or" – Iwelumu walked Lightning closer to DuWayne – "to you, it's half a million pounds."

"Half a million bags? For a horse. Bro, you out your mind!"

"Hold out your hands."

DuWayne's hands shook as he extended them. Lightning dipped his head towards DuWayne's fingers, nostrils flaring. The horse then began a series of sharp sniffs, acquiring DuWayne's scent.

"Flatten them out."

DuWayne did as he was told and Lightning dipped his head further, lips touching DuWayne's palms as he continued sniffing.

"'Wha gwan, bredden? Your horse want to score? Haha!"

"He's picking up your scent. He wants to trust you. I know I don't."

Lightning took two steps towards DuWayne and began licking his overalls.

"Your horse trying to eat me, bro!"

"He's grooming you. Now slowly – put your hand on his neck and rub it."

DuWayne did just that. Lightning edged closer and nuzzled DuWayne's shoulder.

"Don't mess up, yout'" Iwelumu murmured. "It's make or break. Keep rubbing."

"Why am I doing this?"

"Cos you gonna learn to ride, my youth. And in twelve weeks, you're gonna ride at the greatest show on earth."

§

Major Carr advertised online for a groom to replace Annabella but there were no takers. Hardly a surprise: while grooming was the first step on the ladder, it wasn't exactly everyone's equestrian fantasy. Now Carr was worried Janet would walk out, leaving dung un-shovelled, stables un-swept and owners unhappy – all mere weeks before the eyes of the world focused on this estate.

He decided to raise the matter with the board via email. John Iwelumu responded within minutes. If Carr didn't know better, he'd swear Iwelumu wanted the Chairmanship. Or Chairpersonship, or Chair, or whatever he was supposed to call it.

FROM John Iwelumu jiwelumuMBE@rocketmail.com
TO Justin Carr maj.j.carr@palladianHT.com
SUBJECT Re: New Groom

Hi Justin. Thanks for your email. I can spare you the Palladian DEI intern I'm mentoring – DuWayne Anderson. I'm also teaching him to ride, so I'd appreciate it if we can stable Lightning, my eventer for this year's show, at your location.

Let me know if this works.

Best, John

The canny bugger, Carr thought. No other trainer would be allowed to stable their horse here: it'd be like showing a horse at home. But now Iwelumu had this oik working for him, the rest of the board would give him anything.

Iwelumu might have plans, but I've got an ace up my sleeve, reflected Carr. Annabella Amphlett will do my bidding – or else.

§

A month after DuWayne and Lightning moved to the Palladian Estate, neither horse nor rider were happy. DuWayne worked well with Janet when shovelling poo; however, John Iwelumu was also paying her extra to teach DuWayne to ride. And that wasn't going so well. Now Iwelumu was visiting for what he called a "SitRep".

Iwelumu sat in the staff tearoom with an Earl Grey (no milk, no sugar). DuWayne slouched next to him on an easy chair, legs splayed, thumbing through SnapChat. Janet perched on the edge of the table in a big cosy woollen jumper, hands round a steaming mug of tea.

"So Janet. Will DuWayne be the next John Wayne?"

Iwelumu laughed at his own joke. DuWayne didn't even look up.

"Er, well…there may be room for development."

Iwelumu slapped the back of DuWayne's scalp.

"Youth! Put that thing down and pay attention! Janet – tell me what you mean?"

DuWayne looked at Janet with melting puppy eyes.

"DuWayne's been great at ensuring the sanitation of the stable block…."

"You mean man can shovel shit. That's a relief. What about riding?"

"His seat isn't great…."

"And?"

"And his back is like melting jelly and he holds the reins like he's sleeping."

Janet wondered whether another biscuit might calm her down.

"I see." Iwelumu turned to DuWayne. "So – you want back in the pen? Is that it?"

"No massah."

Iwelumu drained his cup of Earl Grey and stood up. Janet saw a vein throb in his temple.

"All right. Now – you" – he pointed at DuWayne. "Don't come that slavery shit with me. You're talking to another black man. I made everything I have with my own two hands."

DuWayne cowered in his chair, anticipating another slap which didn't come.

"So let me tell you – both of you – that I don't tolerate underperformance. You got that?"

Janet and DuWayne nodded in counterpoint.

"Good. You've got three weeks to pull yourself together and learn how to ride. If you fail, you're going back to the pen for the full three. Believe me, I have that power."

"Mr Iwelumu?" Janet murmured. Her face went red as it did in times of stress.

"What is it, Janet?"

"It's not DuWayne's fault. Since coming here, Lightning has been, well, sluggish. He doesn't appear to be settling."

Iwelumu pulled out his wallet and set ten crisp fifty-pound notes on the table.

"Young lady, I am paying you handsomely to train this horse and rider. Whatever you need, you've got it. Only don't give me excuses. Lightning has a bloodline…"

"…that stretches back before the Napoleonic Wars. I know," added Janet.

"So find some other reason. There is nothing wrong with that horse. I'll be back in three weeks, and I want serious improvement: I'm entering DuWayne and Lightning in the three-day event."

Janet wanted to disappear into her tea. The three-day event: cross-country, show-jumping and dressage. If Iwelumu thought some gangbanger from Peckham could mount a horse in two months, let alone compete with lifelong equestrian masters, he wasn't ambitious: he was insane.

Iwelumu's reputation and Lightning's bloodline would get them through pre-qualification automatically – but that only made the prospects of the competition itself more of a daymare of embarrassment for all concerned.

After Iwelumu left, Janet tapped her riding boot against DuWayne's white Nikes.

"Well, cowboy. Looks like we'd better make you John Wayne."

"Safe, girl," cooed DuWayne. "Only never touch my Nikes – and never refer to me in the same breath as them racist bumbaclaat John Wayne, seen?"

§

Later that morning, Major Carr found Annabella in the hall, reading a book. She'd dyed a strand of her golden hair turquoise and gone makeup-free, dressed in what looked like a dark green potato sack.

Carr glanced briefly at the book. Something about de-schooling society, by some foreign Johnny as well. Illic or Billic or whatnot. Pillock, more like.

"Annabella, my dear. Might I have a word?"

Annabella looked up.

"I am not your dear. What is it you want – Major Carr."

"I know. You are our DEI co-ordinator. But that's what I want to talk to you about."

"Go on, Justin."

"It's John Iwelumu," Carr stuttered. "I – er – well, basically, I think he's trying to take over the Palladians and I have to stop him."

"Oh do you?" Annabella asked, returning to her book. "That wouldn't be the stock response of a patriarchal white male to the threat of a black man on his territory, would it?"

Carr stared at her.

"Look here, my girl. I am not having some dreadful oik from Peckham competing in my trials."

"Well then, you'd better do something about it, hadn't you?"

Carr was about to go down the "you work for me" route, but it was no use: Annabella slammed her book shut and slipped away. Carr sat heavily on a sofa and stared at a painting of the Charge of the Light Brigade. Thirty years of army life had not been in vain: he knew just how to hit Iwelumu where it hurt. And now he stood ready to strike.

§

Three weeks later, a miracle had happened – if you call riding eight hours each day and watching videos about balance, posture and seat all night miraculous. DuWayne was able to walk from the stables and trot Lightning round the manège. A long way from dressage, but it was a start.

That left Janet with two problems. First, she had five weeks to turn DuWayne into a competition-level rider. Secondly, Lightning: he'd been acting more like a superannuated dray horse than a half-million pound thoroughbred. He stood on his hooves when he should jump: his head dipped when he should hold it high.

"Nice work today, DuWayne."

Janet grabbed Lightning's bridle as horse and rider came in from another trudge round the manège.

"I told you man could do it. I was Prince of the Ends till someone chatted shit and I got banged."

"I'm sure," Janet said, holding Lightning as DuWayne made an uneasy descent. "But it takes years. And Lightning's not helping. He seems continually out of sorts."

"I'll fix Lightning. Trust me. Just show me the moves and I'll bust 'em, seen?"

Janet smiled. "Dressage isn't hip-hop, DuWayne."

But DuWayne had drifted off, singing about eyes on that girl size while hitting up numbers on his phone.

§

At an early hour the next morning when no civvy would stir, Major Justin Carr rose, shaved, dressed and made his way to the stables with an industrial-sized dose of Instant Magic.

He'd acquired the well-known horse tranquiliser on the sly from an old army vet he'd served with in Scotland. The chap owed him several favours after Carr saved his bacon when the vet swapped the brigadier's burgundy for some Buckfast Tonic Wine.

If anyone were to urine-sample Lightning, they'd find giant rivers of ketamine in his piss. But then, reflected Carr, that urchin DuWayne probably sold this stuff in London's slums. Blaming him would be simple.

Carr mixed a whopping dollop of Instant Magic into Lightning's feed. The horse was getting a taste for it – unlike Carr and modernity, which he wished would just go back to London where it belonged.

§

The next time he visited, John Iwelumu got a surprise. Though Lightning was still slow and groggy, DuWayne was able to sit up and trot him round the manège, even managing to coax him over the lower obstacles with much hesitation.

"I see progress," Iwelumu told Janet afterwards. "But not enough. I'm a winner – and winners win. So here's the deal: get DuWayne on the podium next month and I'll give you a hundred thousand pounds."

"You'd better keep your money," Janet snapped. "Unless we find out what's wrong with Lightning, all bets are off."

DuWayne trotted up and slid off Lightning's saddle like a pro.

"See that? Getting better, innit? Like old Marley used to sing – "*every little ting / Gonna be alright*" – aiiite?"

Iwelumu's impervious features said otherwise.

"I'll be back the night before the trials. I expect you to be ready."

Iwelumu left DuWayne clutching Lightning by the bridle, one hand on Janet's shoulder for support.

"You said you'd fix Lightning. We're finished if we can't make him faster."

"Man can't do every ting lickety-split. Specially not here, seen?"

"DuWayne, you aren't going to do anything horrible, are you?"

"Jus' trust me, girl," smiled DuWayne. "Now, what you doing after work?"

§

The week of the trials arrived in all their pomp – cameras, journalists, spectators; the sponsors, food vendors and horse owners. On the Friday, Lightning ran the cross-country speedier than the grave. DuWayne managed to hold on as they shot round the estate's perimeter, clear and inside the optimum time. And that's when the impossible happened.

Where other riders urged their horses on with whips and spurs, DuWayne yelled something unintelligible. Lightning ran even faster and finished with no time penalties. If that evening's mandatory urine sample would eventually reveal Lightning to have ingested a pharmacopoeia hitherto unknown to either man or horse, then for that moment, at least, John Iwelumu was ecstatic. Major Carr, predictably enough, appeared less than pleased.

The Saturday brought less good news. No doubt sore from the previous day's exertions, DuWayne and Lightning came far down the leader board in show-jumping. As before, DuWayne managed to tease Lightning through some of the obstacles, but he knocked poles off left, right and centre. As a result, the judges awarded DuWayne more faults than a tectonic plate.

That left Sunday – and the dressage competition. And in this, DuWayne's performance was wondrous. After a morning of horses dancing to everything from Wagner to the Bee Gees, Janet felt pure horror suffuse her soul when she heard DuWayne being announced:

"*Mr DuWayne Anderson rides Lightning, a thoroughbred stallion owned by Mr John Iwelumu, to the tune of T-Pain's 'Grrl I am Sprung' in the F-U baby yehyeh remix by Junkie XL Krew.*"

Horse and rider entered the ring. Where Janet had coached DuWayne to execute a simple square halt, Lightning had other ideas. Such as a perfect piaffe followed by a canter pirouette that led to a series of flying changes, those most impossible of dressage manoeuvres. All to a drill rap remixed by drugged-out Dutch DJs.

Needless to say the audience erupted. The judges scored nines and tens, encouraged by whispers from Annabella about DuWayne's adverse circumstances. When rosette time came, it found DuWayne on the podium clutching his floral facsimile like a politician with street cred – as if such a thing existed.

Afterwards, John Iwelumu approached Janet and DuWayne.

"I'm keeping my promise. One hundred thousand pounds each. What's more, I want you both to work for me."

DuWayne kissed Janet on the cheek.

"I owe it all to you. I mean it. Thank you."

Annabella Amphlett's career in DEI took off after DuWayne's miraculous performance. Radio Four's *Farming Today* did a special on equestrian diversity featuring Annabella, after which she got a *Guardian* column. And if, in time, DuWayne revealed to Janet that Lightning's stellar gallop had been chemically assisted – and his dressage inspired by magic mushrooms – then media coverage about the Palladian's DEI initiative, riding's new star from the Peckham ghetto and John Iwelumu's triumph as an enlightened horse owner made up for any wrongdoing. Indeed, the glowing media reports made it impossible for the judges to rescind DuWayne's prizes once the drugs were discovered in Lightning's system.

As for Major Carr, one week after the trials he sat late in his study watching the sunset. He laid a hand on his father's cigarette case, then examined the portrait of King Charles III over the door. Maybe it was time to retire. But if he retired, he would do so knowing there would be a corner of this world, however small – perhaps just this office – that would forever remain the England he had loved and known, even if, in reality, that world was gone for good.

For One Night Only

Herbert Smith checked the invitation in his breast pocket: it was still there, even though he'd checked it was still there so many times he'd risked losing it. He was surprised to have been invited to a premiere – presumably some PR called his agent asking her to find a couple of meat puppets to fill the room.

This was the first after-party he'd been invited to in ten years as a Thespian: a full decade, not a single premiere. Thus far, his professional life must have delighted his family, since they'd never wanted him to be an actor.

Herbert was thirty-two. Since leaving university, he'd drunk deep of youth's glorious trials: bit parts; the odd voice-over; even four speaking parts in films, two of which finished on the cutting-room floor.

To earn a living, he stacked shelves in a supermarket. Lines of beige metal at three a.m., waiting for Herbert to deposit another flatpack of stewed tomatoes or leaden bags of flour that leaked white powder through their outer packaging – an actor's nose in reverse, if you will.

He'd also earned cash pulling pints, waiting tables and temping. So far he'd never done porn or driven a taxi – but yes, he'd do the former before the latter. Still, he'd found enough acting work to justify carrying on: but not enough to make his way.

The worst thing in Herbert's life, however, wasn't his own failure. It was the existence of a man who shared his name, Herbert Smith. And worse than that, this Bert Smith – as he styled himself – was an actor. A wildly successful one at that.

Famous Bert Smith was two years younger than our Herbert. His angular features first graced screens as CIA agent Craig Frank in *Undercover*, then as the male lead in some successful "Hollywood-meets-art" films. Bert had stolen Herbert's name and run away to live his dreams, from features in style mags to a trophy girlfriend and football-pitch-sized house in LA.

Herbert first encountered his homonym seven years ago, shortly after being promoted to frozen-vegetables manager at the supermarket. Taking his regulation ten-minute coffee break one night, Herbert flopped into the filthy staff canteen with a cup of pseudo-espresso from a hulking, outdated drinks machine.

He sat down and ran his hands over his face. Another four hours of throwing sacks of vegetables into a freezer before he could go home and dream sad dreams of stardom. Across the room, a figure in butcher's overalls sat masticating the remnants of whatever snack it had just ingested. After some time, a voice emerged from its mouth to break the silence.

"What you working here for, then?"

Herbert recognised the voice as that of Jon Postlethwaite, relief night manager in the butchery department.

"What do you mean? I need the money, like everyone else."

"Not anymore you don't, does ya?"

Postlethwaite grinned and held up an open copy of *The Sun* so Herbert could see the headline on the showbiz page:

BERT'S A DEAD CERT!

Best known to audiences on the box as CIA hunk Craig Frank, actor Bert Smith (23) has just inked a deal to play the lead in Kate Callat's *Neck Romance* – a story of vampires, love and intrigue in a big city morgue. Beefcake Bert, who hails from Tiverton but now lives in LA, has recently been spotted with glamorous Model / Actress / Whatever Querida Chingar. Rumour has it they're house-hunting in Bel Air....

The article pictured Querida diving off a boat in the Gulf of Mexico, perfect thighs glistening in the early morning sun. Herbert slumped back on the tearoom sofa and raised his eyes to the fluorescent strip lights above.

This was the ultimate indignity. Failure was cosy enough, most of the time: if no one knew your name, you had nothing to lose. But to watch a contemporary live your dreams, thinking it could be you, and one who had the same name…*he that steals from me my good name steals something more precious than riches….*

Later that week, as Herbert shuffled down Tottenham Court Road towards another unpromising audition, he looked up to find Bert Smith's six-pack staring back at him from a huge underwear billboard. A few days later, he picked up a stained copy of *GQ* in a dentist's waiting room. On the back cover, a wryly smiling Bert Smith was advertising timepieces: "ROLEX. BERT SMITH'S CHOICE".

Herbert passed his nights not creeping the boards as a Thespian, but tossing frozen peas into metal sarcophagi to earn a living, a monotony broken by occasional calls to do corporate videos or auditions for parts he knew would go to whoever was banging the producer.

Then one day his luck turned. He got a proper speaking part. One of those slice-of-life TV dramas set in a hospital. Herbert played a male nurse of dubious sexual orientation – fitting, given his total lack of action since a confused fumble while half-drunk at a wedding years ago.

He was guaranteed at least ten episodes because they'd written the script that far. Herbert remembered how his agent's jowls jiggled with excitement when she said he'd got the role. She bought him lunch in the same Italian restaurant they'd visited when she signed him. As the wine flowed, so did the promises. Hollywood. Product sponsorship in Asia. Nothing was too fantastic after a third glass of Frascati and fifteen per cent of a thousand pounds per episode.

§

A week after that lunch, Herbert found himself in a loaned dinner suit clutching the invitation to this after-party for some film premiere – the usual Hollywood summertime schlock: tits, bums and saving the world from environmental disaster.

He approached the panelled oak entrance of the hotel where the party was being held. A PR person ticked off names, glad-handing, air-kissing and smiling welcomes at entrants passing through her spiritual meat grinder.

"Herbert Smith?"

Herbert nodded.

"But you go by Bert, right?"

"Well, actually, I—"

"Not another word. Let me know if the paps are bugging you and we'll get you out via the kitchen, OK? Where's Querida? I'm sooo pleased you could make it, darling!" she gushed, enveloping him in an awkward hug.

She disengaged herself from the hug and snapped her fingers. A young man with a floppy fringe wearing a black suit leapt forward from behind a plant pot.

"Take charge of the line, William," she said. "And do me a favour. Put Bert Smith down as 'VIP attended', OK?"

William the nascent PR flack nodded his assent.

"Love your films," he wibbled before his boss guided Herbert into the main room.

Herbert was flying and shitting himself all at once. He spotted Mick Jagger chatting to a model young enough to be his granddaughter. Naomi Campbell, the image of statuesque perfection in a tan-and-black gown. All of life was here – or what passed for life in the parallel universe of celebritydom. A world hermetically sealed against the likes of Herbert Smith – until today.

"There are sooo many people you need to meet. I thought you were based in LA," the PR crooned, steering Herbert through the crowd.

A waiter brought drinks. The PR lady – Herbert couldn't read her nametag, she kept moving so fast – handed him a champagne flute and took one herself. Herbert necked a long swallow. It had been years since he'd tasted champagne: this hospital series would just about pay down his credit card. Almost.

He tried to guess the PR woman's name from the scribble on her nametag. Linda or Liana or something.

"Listen, Linda—"

"It's Liana, Bert. But whatever."

"Liana. I must tell you. I'm not—"

"HAAAARVEY! Oh my God! I thought you were in New York! Let me introduce you to Bert Smith! Yes, I know – in London! What a surprise!"

The PR dervish released Herbert and dashed towards an overweight man in his late fifties with a greying, unkempt beard. The man wore an immaculate dinner jacket and garish silk tie.

"Hello Bert. Pleasure to meet you. I'm Harvey Linitz – producer of tonight's film for Sony Pictures."

Herbert took another gulp of champagne, feeling an overwhelming urge to dive into the glass and swim away even as his pulse skipped with possibility.

"Hello," Herbert croaked, Harvey's hand smothering his with a car-crusher shake.

"So what you working on?" Harvey asked, looking him up and down. "Hey, you've lost weight, right? Love the new hair colour – quite the departure!"

Herbert grimaced. Truth time.

"Well, I—" He froze. Someone had stuffed something in the breast pocket of his jacket.

A woman brushed past him looking like Marilyn Monroe in *Some Like It Hot*. She carried a tray of cigarettes and chewing gum. She winked at him and pointed to his breast pocket, then turned away. Herbert assumed she'd given him a packet of gum. But it was a note – he'd read it later.

Harvey Linitz looked at Herbert.

"Come on, Bert. I know your agent. You can tell me."

Herbert smiled and was about to utter the greatest lie ever told outside the bedroom when Liana the PR ching-chinged her champagne glass for silence.

"Thank you for attending this premiere of *A Prophet's Tears*. I know we all have a lot of suits to hug and air to kiss" – a ripple of laughter, though no one found her remark remotely funny – "but before we get going, I wanted to ask Harvey Linitz to say a few words."

Applause, then all eyes on Linitz, who stood next to Herbert. Now he really wanted to disappear.

"Thank you, Liana. And thank you, everyone, for coming tonight. You know, I could talk to you for hours about this movie. If you've got any money, I probably already have…" – a few grunts of unamused recognition – "…but let me say this: I'm proud of what we've done. It'll gross millions, sure. But this isn't about money. It's about that moment when you turn around and say, like the great European filmmakers of yore: *je suis cinéaste*."

Harvey's Brooklyn accent maimed the French phrase. Herbert glanced at the note the Marilyn lookalike had stuffed in his pocket. A mobile phone number scrawled above a single sentence that promised him a spectacularly vulgar sexual favour.

Herbert looked up as Harvey Linitz resumed speaking:

"ART!" Harvey bellowed. "ART! That's why we're here. It's true – everyone knows I've made money for my investors. But I never lost sight of why we're doing this. Ladies and gentlemen, we live for art."

Harvey put an arm around Herbert's shoulder. "As proof of how much we love art in movies, I have with me England's most talented young actor. You will know him from *Neck Romance*. Or *Undercover*. Or maybe you've just seen him in those underwear commercials" – more unamused laughter. "But ladies and gentlemen, my friend Bert Smith here is an artist, above all. A true Thespian. He's not just in it to make dunghills of moolah and end up in the Chateau Marmont with six strippers and a slagheap of cocaine. No: he's laboured for his craft. And to prove it, he's going to recite Shakespeare for us."

Right, here goes, thought Herbert. My moment. He clutched his glass in both hands, that note from the Monroe impersonator twisted between anxious fingers.

"Thank you, Harvey." Herbert smiled at his new friend in a facsimile of the affection veterans who'd shared a foxhole must feel for each other: "It would be my pleasure."

Herbert began declaiming the soliloquy from Act V of *Othello*.

"*Soft you, a word or two before you go. / I have done the state some service, and they know't…*"

The audience listened in silence. Herbert's eyes floated around the room as a voice that seemed not to be his ran through the verses – only it was him. This was real. His hour had come.

Mick Jagger moodily sipped champagne and checked his phone […] *of one whose subdued eyes* […] / *Drops tears as fast as the Arabian trees / Their medicinable gum* […] Naomi Campbell rummaged in her clutch, poking her assistant and gesturing inside her bag, *Set you down this, / And say besides that in Aleppo once*, as he reached the thundering climax, there was first silence, then a geyser of applause.

Harvey Linitz enveloped Herbert in a bearhug. "I don't know who you are, kid," Linitz yelled in his ear over the applause, "but that was wonderful."

Herbert released himself from Harvey's crushing embrace. He may never be famous. He might stack frozen peas for the rest of his days. But tonight, for one night only, he was swinging the world by its tail. And maybe that was enough.

Flare-up!

When he got that text, Hamish Reilly was scrolling through social media photos of Bunny on his phone. Back in the long ago, he used to sleep with Bunny when they were students at Oxford. Now she lived alone in a South London terrace, obsessed with Candy Crush and posting political memes on Facebook, while he, Hamish, ruled the universe.

Or that's how it seemed: if he didn't rule the universe, at least he ruled a galaxy known as Manhattan, with New York at its core and Shanghai and Mumbai wafting around like dwarf planets for his pleasure.

Hamish thwacked his phone shut. He needed to leave. That text was from his private security advisors. And it told him the world was about to end.

§

Alberto Morelos stopped his tractor. Up in the hills above Cereté, life was hard. Berto left the Colombian school system at fourteen and went to plant potatoes with his dad. Not exactly Beverly Hills – but Berto tried to put his faith in God. Sure, he'd dreamed of being a football star, even tried out for Independiente Medellín when he was twelve. And he still wanted America. The cars. The houses. The food. Maybe one day, maybe….

Whenever the boredom of life as a farmer confronted him, he tried to count his blessings: Maria and their daughter Estrella; his family, the farm. Pacifico beers at the Casa Rosa in town; potatoes swapped with other farmers for beans or meat – stuff a man really needs. But that didn't stop him dreaming of Lamborghinis and cocktail bars in idle moments.

Berto sniffed the air. There was something different, some electric tang that said evil was coming. He coughed his ancient tractor into life and sloughed down through the mud towards his family, wanting to make sure they were safe. He always trusted his instincts. Something dark was headed their way….

§

Sprinting to the parking lot, Hamish jumped behind the wheel of his Tesla and stamped on the accelerator.

His security people said he had ten minutes till the news broke. When he got to his apartment on Gertrude Street a helicopter hovered twenty feet above his building. He'd already texted Blossom to meet him on the roof. The security guys would pick up his kids, Timon and Humbert, from Yale and get them to the family's safe farm in the Catskills.

As the helicopter pulled up, Hamish looked across at Blossom, his wife, and wondered why he'd bothered including her in his Armageddon plan. Christened Tanqueray after her mum's favourite gin, she answered to Blossom thanks to the blush her mother acquired from said gin. Hamish had met her at the Gotham Book Mart when she was promoting her first novel, a slice-of-life comedy about girls dating bankers after the '07 crash.

He'd assumed she was rich and she'd assumed he was desperate to get married so no one would think he was a homo. She was right and he was wrong. Five years later, he found himself the father of two boys and $3,000,000 poorer thanks to the purchase of said apartment on Gertrude Street.

Hamish glanced across the cramped cockpit as they headed for the Catskills. Whatever he'd seen in Blossom was gone. Subjectively, she was beautiful, rich and skinny. Objectively, they barely spoke and hadn't had sex in eight years.

But none of that mattered. What mattered was kicking off ninety-three million miles away. A gigantic solar flare set to knock out every electronic device on earth. And they needed to land fast so they didn't crash when that flare hit. Although well over fifty, death still scared the shit out of Hamish.

§

Out in space, shockwaves shot from the sun, out past Mercury. Gamma rays, X-rays, light and heat. As Berto kissed Maria and picked up Estrella for a cuddle, those shockwaves reached Venus.

And by the time Hamish and Blossom touched down at their farm northeast of Woodstock, Earth's ionosphere tasted the first shifting hints of the electromagnetic radiation bomb that was just about to strike.

Hamish disembarked from the heli and greeted the ex-Special Forces operatives he'd hired on retainer for protection during precisely this kind of disaster scenario. He scurried across the landing pad's enormous H as the sky erupted in light: symphonies of green and orange and red, flashes falling in curtains against the empty azure of space as if every angel and devil decided to visit Earth at once.

His two boys waited for him in front of the bunker. Humbert, the elder, held the hand of some underfed, spotty girl.

"Dad, meet Natasha. I wanted her to come with me so—"

Hamish sized her up as a possibility for an off night for himself, but not a fit consort for his son.

"No way, H," he said. "Girlfriends are out. She has to go."

Hamish clicked his fingers and two black-clad former Navy SEALs grabbed Natasha, who yelped as she was shoved into an armoured vehicle and, Hamish presumed, driven to the gate of their property two miles away. He never found out what happened to her, though.

"Everything's ready, sir. The hydroponics are activated and the generators are up. This way, sir."

The family followed their burly retainer down a set of concrete stairs to a door. Hamish stepped forward and peered into a retinal scanner. The door swished open to reveal a long chamber with rooms left and right. Everything was in order – the exercise room; separate sleeping quarters; the dining area, kitchen and all.

Hamish was pleased to see the Picasso he loved to brag about perched on the wall. Family was one thing – but that Picasso was something else: *Le gourmet*, from 1901. Eighty million if it was a penny, and worth every cent.

§

"Stay here. I'm gonna check on my parents."

"What is this thing? *¡Dios mio¡* Berto, I'm scared."

"Who knows? God's anger with the world. But we'll survive. Trust in Him, *mi vida*."

Berto tried to call his parents but the cellphones were down. He got in his tractor and sparked the engine, but it wouldn't turn. So he jumped out of the cab and started walking, ready to troop the five kilometres to his parents' shack. A long way from Beverly Hills.

The mystery of those lights lit up the afternoon sky above the Andes. Unknown to Berto, it was the same everywhere: fingers stabbed at screens in London, frustrated in mid-swipe: ancient desktop computers mouldering in Tashkent offices gave a spark, then expired. A world that relied on electronic brains linked to other electronic brains had come to a juddering halt.

§

Hamish stared at his Picasso on the wall like some trinket on a market stall. The last briefing he'd caught before the internet went dead said every global market had tanked – but who knew for sure, now there was no internet?

He heard the generators burbling in the service room. At least they were working, giving him and Blossom and the boys light and heat forty feet underground. Across the bunker's main room, Blossom fiddled with a recipe book as if this whole thing were some dystopian weekend in the Hamptons.

Didn't she understand? Did the boys? Any object that relied on electromagnetism to function had just had a heart attack and died. Even if they got the power back up, all laptops, engines, medical equipment, machinery of any kind were fucked. And the more they relied on microprocessors and chips, the more fucked they were.

Timon had his arms round Humbert, who sobbed like a six-year-old denied a plate of fries. Hamish took a step towards them.

"Don't you come near me! I've always hated you! You sent Natasha to her death! You fucking pig! Fuck you – and your money!"

Humbert threw a heavy vase at his father. Hamish had bought that vase at an exhibition in the Bowery to impress some supermodel a few years ago. He ducked and it hit the far wall, smashing into a thousand pieces, give or take. The two guards by the outer door didn't even flinch when it smashed. Maybe they would have if they'd known it was worth $800,000.

Hamish opened the drinks cabinet and poured himself a many-fingered tumbler of Hine Cigar Reserve. Looked like their first night back in the Stone Age would be a long one.

§

A few hours later, the earth turned in incomparable stillness as nature intended. Half of its eight billion human cargo was unable to sleep or eat or rest, such was their state of utter incomprehension. Life as they knew it – the rubbernecking, device-obsessed, constantly-message-checking life – had vanished.

The world's governments – or, let's be honest, the world *government* – was slow to respond. Without their usual machinery of the internet, judging public sentiment became impossible. How would people survive without Bluetooth headphones, voice-activated browser bots or smart watches?

Children grew depressed, no longer able to make twitchy movements to propel some pixellated avatar around a bleeping screen. Needless to say, the churches remained empty. In those first few days, no one gave any thought to their souls. Not yet, anyway.

§

Alberto Morelos held Estrella and Maria in a hug. They were cooking *asado,* Argentine-style BBQ, at his parents' place. His dad strummed a guitar as bottles of beer cooled in the water-butt at the side of their house. Their dog, a real Andes mongrel of a hundred breeds, gambolled around waiting for scraps.

Berto released his family and turned his attention to the food – sausages, steaks and vegetables. Six giant potatoes wrapped in foil rested on a rack above the meat as it spat and hissed fat onto the glowing charcoal beneath.

OK, so they couldn't run the tractor or get to market. But they had candles. They had water. Playing centre-forward for Chelsea or sitting in a hot tub in the Hamptons mattered less to Berto now. In fact, dreams of stardom were the last thing on his mind. Finally, he was happy.

§

"I want a divorce!"

Blossom's cheeks streamed tears as she confronted Hamish. This is not what he'd paid $10,000,000 for. Not once you considered the cost of the bunker and gun-toting goons, the supplies and the thousands of litres of water, the pallets of high-end Meals Ready to Eat featuring fully organic produce. After just forty-eight hours back together, it seemed Blossom had worked out how much she hated him. And so had the boys.

"You complete fucking twat! How could you throw our son's girlfriend out? Or did you want her for yourself? Don't think I don't know, Hamish!"

Humbert had his DJ headphones on, lost in his own world. Timon lay cloistered on his bed, probably consoling himself furiously as every man is rumoured to have done since wrist joints revealed their more pleasurable purpose. One of the goons made a signal, giving Hamish the opportunity to avoid answering Blossom.

"Sir? Our intel is the power should be back up soon. We're also hearing secondary reports, sir…."

Why can't these people speak normally, for Christ's sake?

"What do you mean?"

The guard coughed into his Kevlar mitt, a superfluous Heckler & Koch submachine gun strapped across his back.

"Well, sir, I am hearing the world's data centres are wiped."

Hamish thanked him and turned back to his family. No more social media. No more credit histories. No more TINDR, online tax reminders, purchase histories. No ads assuming he had erectile dysfunction, needed a mail-order bride or wanted to wear a T-shirt pledging his allegiance to some washed-up singer or politician. Thank God. But who thanked God anymore? No one Hamish knew, that's for sure.

Hamish twigged that, in all probability, all his non-physical wealth had gone too. Not good. Not good at all. He turned to Blossom:

"You want a divorce? Have one. And take half of everything. Only there is no 'everything'. We're ruined!"

"Ruined?"

At the mention of the word, Humbert removed his headphones. Seeing his paramour banished was nothing compared to the fear that he might have to seek some form of gainful employment. He leapt up and scuttled off to find his brother.

§

After electricity and the internet returned, so did normality – but it stood at an obtuse angle to what came prior to the catastrophe, if that's what you'd call it.

Hamish and Blossom, now barely on speaking terms, chose to stay in their bunker with their sons until the "all clear" was given. One morning three months later, after he'd savoured his usual sweet, nutty espresso made from freshly ground Jamaican Blue Mountain beans, Hamish stood behind Timon in the bunker watching his son scrolling through a social media feed.

"What in God's name is that?"

His finger stabbed at an image of a near-naked woman on the screen. She appeared to be fellating a fire hydrant.

"She's an influencer, Dad. No one's using social media after what happened. I guess three months is enough to change people's habits."

"But why is she—"

"Oh – that! Well, none of the influencers are making money anymore. So they are basically offering, um, favours to people who follow them. It sucks, TBH."

Hamish wondered briefly how to contact the young woman whose tongue writhed against the hydrant, then dismissed the idea after reflecting that if the situation sucked then so, clearly, did she. But the last thing he needed was more ammo for his wife's lawyers.

"Anyway. I'm off to do some reading. See ya, Dad!"

And with that, Timon picked up a dogeared book from the coffee table. Hamish noticed the title: *Tools for Conviviality.* That's not the kind of reading that'll get him a job, Hamish mused as Timon headed for the bunkroom he shared with his brother.

Hamish stood like an icon, transfixed by the woman on Timon's phone twerking against the hydrant as if participating in the vulgar jissom rite of some obscure religion. An ad for a reality TV show popped up on Timon's cellphone as Hamish watched her. Said advertisement promised the show would reveal live footage of divorced couples sleeping with each other on their first dates. Hamish decided he needed another espresso, only this time with a belt of Hine as a livener. He headed for the kitchen.

§

Back in the hills above Cereté, Berto finished his lunchtime sandwich. For him, this "disaster" was like a pleasant break with the family. Like normal, without work. And now things were back, only better than before. Scoring in the World Cup? A distant dream compared to the peace and contentment which, day by day, had slowly infused his soul.

He'd been checking the football scores and fan message boards on his cellphone – not that he posted much anymore. He put his phone away and got the tractor in gear. The potato crop he'd planted six weeks ago was coming along nicely. Thirty acres of yield would see them through the next few months, thank God.

When he got home his mother had chicken and potato *ajiaco* stew waiting for him. Why they hadn't asked his parents to live with them before the sun erupted was a mystery: everything was better now they lived as one. Something changed when they lost power – life became enhanced, as if they now knew what mattered.

"How was your day, *mi hijo?*"

"Fine. We'll be ready to harvest in a couple of months, no more."

He kissed her and held her tight. He didn't worry about her and Dad, not now they'd sold up in the city and moved back home. They had enough money – plus the terror of those lights in the sky showed him all things were the will of God.

Berto finished his plate of stew as Maria came in. She'd walked Estrella back from nursery: another change. No more cars for everything – no need. Walking was better. Slower, maybe. But with his parents around for help, Maria wasn't as rushed. They were blessed.

§

After the authorities gave the all-clear, Blossom moved back into the apartment on Gertrude Street while Hamish remained at their farm. Despite describing themselves to friends and online as "happily separated and sharing parenting of their two tremendous sons", they hated each other to the depths of their tripes.

Such mutual antipathy was not improved by the handwritten note Hamish picked up in the bunker shortly after Blossom returned to New York:

Dear Mom and Dad,

We reject the life you had planned for us. No more Yale followed by starter jobs on Wall Street. We want real life – so we're heading out on the road and don't know when we'll be back. But we'll get in touch.

Six months? A year? As long as it takes. We're going to New Mexico in a motorhome. Sorry about stealing the rations but I guess you don't need them now.

By the way, you might find this book useful.

Love, T and H

Under the note Hamish found a copy of a book called *The Technical Society* by some Frenchman named Ellul. It was over 400 pages, wasn't about money or sex and didn't have any illustrations, so Hamish was unlikely even to glance at it.

As he stood contemplating his family's dissolution, his cellphone rang. It was his private banker, Nick Rosso.

"Nick? How's things? How's the portfolio – recovering?"

"Uh, that's kind of why I'm calling, Hamish."

"What is it?"

Hamish listened as Rosso confirmed the worst. The data wipe and subsequent breaches had left him with nothing in the bank. Nothing in his retirement plan. No Roth, no 401 (k). Nada, zip, zilch. He would have to sell Gertrude Street and the artwork. Every bit of it – and these days, no one was buying. Everyone who'd had any coin was the same: wiped out.

He left a voice message with Blossom – who'd changed her greeting to make herself sound more perky for potential suitors. Quite the change from the lemon-featured harridan he'd come to know during the course of their marriage. Then he took his last $5,000 he didn't have out of the bank via his credit card and headed for New Mexico, hoping either to find his sons or enlightenment of some kind.

§

In the end, Hamish found neither. So he returned to the farm where he lived alone for a spell, eating down the rations and spending almost nothing while the sale of Gertrude Street – for less than a quarter of the 3,000,000 he'd originally paid for it – went through. Blossom moved to New Jersey after their apartment sold but soon discovered Camden was a different proposition to the Lower West Side.

One day she pitched up at the farm with two suitcases of clothes and a new hair-do.

"I'm willing to try again," she said.

Hamish brought her into the bunker and they sat in silence for a while, contemplating that Picasso, the one thing he refused to sell.

"We've got less than 2,000,000 left. Chump change. The kind of money a suburban dentist retires on. I understand if you want to leave. I've failed you."

Blossom put her arms around him.

"You haven't failed. This is just the start of something better."

Hamish looked her over. There was a radiance about her, a light in her eyes he'd never seen before. She kissed him and picked up a family photo from the coffee table that showed the boys nestled between them on a sofa back on Gertrude Street. Timon and Humbert were smiling but looking away from the camera, while Hamish and Blossom did all they could to look like model parents.

"Those boys will be back soon," she said. "And when they come back, they'll live here, with us. Work this land, grow crops and raise families. And we'll love them like never before."

Hamish put his arms around her and they held each other tight. So it was that a random act of interplanetary nuclear physics managed to achieve what tens of millions of dollars, extensive therapy and every material object under the sun had failed to deliver. Hamish and Blossom had found the truth, and each other – at last.

Crunch Time for the Pheasant

Martin Hugginson was an ordinary man who dreamed of the extraordinary. Everything about him was average: his looks, his height, the condition of his hypothalamus – in fact, the size and condition of every organ. Yes, including that one.

Unusually for someone so ambitious, he was also a nice boy. You know – get a job, get married, have children. Make his parents proud and have a nice life. After he graduated from the University of Coventry with a lower second-class degree in psychology ("very creditable," his tutor said) he began casting about for a career.

A few months of botched applications and failed interviews followed. Then he spotted an advertisement for a junior data assistant at the National Statistics Office in Nuneaton, Warwickshire.

"That'll do me," Martin thought.

§

The National Statistics Office (NSO) was housed in one of those 1960s blocks which always seem to be located near a station. Wherever you live in the world, you've seen one like it: grey, filthy, rectangular windows and a flat roof. The kind of place that, when you pass in a train, you wonder who or what dwells within its walls. Somewhere that looks more like a filing cabinet than a place of work.

§

I should have told you Martin got the job, but you probably guessed. After all, junior data assistant at the National Statistics Office hardly sets your hair on fire, does it? A lower second in psychology from Coventry University was more than enough to perform as required.

Martin's job consisted of handling data enquiries from the public and government departments. He had twenty days holiday on top of public holidays, a final-salary pension and £22,000 per year – much less than other graduates. But Martin didn't care. It was a start.

§

The NSO's Nuneaton site hid a secret. At its heart there lay a grass quadrangle. Perhaps the architects imagined an oasis for those crunching numbers inside; a place to have lunch or chat to colleagues. Maybe even contemplate boredom-related self-harm.

It was almost always deserted given the amount of rain pouring down nine months of the year. Four rotting-wet wooden park benches faced each other, one on each side; on two sides, waste bins for lunchers to put sandwich wrappers in. A one-legged pheasant wandered about as well.

No one knew how the pheasant got there, or why it didn't fly away. Sometimes staff spotted it venturing up to the roof, where it would squawk and cackle. But it never left. Most likely, it fed on any worm unfortunate enough to poke its head through the grass, or on scraps of sandwich tossed to it by employees. Maybe someone was secretly feeding it drugs, which explained why it didn't go anywhere.

Its feathers were dark red and it had yellow eyes. It compensated for its ambulatory disability by being the loudest bird Martin had ever heard in his life.

§

Martin's boss welcomed him on his first day with a nondescript handshake and a brief grin. Paul Harfrow was two years away from statutory retirement and had worked in this building for thirty-four years. He'd long ago settled here, and it had settled into him, his bulbous form weighed down by a Herculean gut that preceded him everywhere.

"This is your desk," he told Martin, pointing at a dark plastic-looking table, eight feet long and four feet wide with an old-fashioned computer on it. "We'll look at what you'll be doing later."

§

Martin was given a week to read through the induction manual, make sure he knew where things were on the server, and hide in the toilets when he couldn't take being at his desk anymore. He undertook these non-tasks in a giant enclosure under strip lights, then went home and ate sausages or beans with potatoes – mashed, boiled, fried. Sometimes he ate a curry.

Back in the office, the nearest employee to him sat twenty yards away. He was called Trevor. Trevor was bald on top with long, unkempt grey hair that stuck out at the sides and ran down his neck. He was quite old, about the same age as Paul Harfrow. Martin had noticed Trevor dozing off after lunch. He smelled of stale beer and cigarette smoke.

After a week of surfing the internet and listening to pheasant squawks, Martin started wondering if this was the right job for him. But then, that Friday morning, he met Fenella Clarke. And someone gave him something to do – at last.

§

Fenella Clarke was a slash of scarlet on the used cellophane of the National Statistics Office. She worked as executive assistant to Tom Taylor, the top dog in this place. They looked like a couple out of an office furniture ad: Taylor, a trim man in his late fifties with dark charcoal suits, a white shirt, and blue tie; Fenella in a pencil skirt and two-inch heels. She had a long wavy perm, deep crimson lipstick, and big glasses with thin frames. She was young, like Martin.

Martin found her unbearably sexy. So much so that when Tom Taylor came to his desk that Friday morning to greet him as the new recruit, he looked down and away. Even though Fenella did no more than stand behind her boss holding a tablet computer. But when you're twenty-two and your hormones are on fire, that's enough.

§

"Settling in all right, are we, er, Martin? Did Paul give you enough to do?"

Martin could tell by the way Taylor looked at him he was expected to bullshit. So he did: "Oh yes, thank you, Mr Taylor."

The two men shook hands. Tom Taylor smelled of soap – reassuringly.

"Good. Well, there's something I'd like you to do for me."

"Certainly, Mr Taylor – just name it."

The pheasant crowed in the quadrangle down below.

"Bloody bird. Still, you'll get used to it," said Taylor with the kind of quick smile that suggested he never had. "Now look. The Department of Health is asking for a multi-variant analysis of health outcomes for all children born between 2000 and 2015 split out by region and gender, parental income, and marital status. I know it's a lot to ask, but Fenella here will give you a hand, all right?"

Martin said it was fine by him. In particular, working with Fenella was especially fine.

"Very good. Oh – and I need to see something by four p.m. today, OK?"

Martin nodded like a marionette on speed and Taylor was gone. Fenella Clarke waited until her boss was out of earshot then sat down in Martin's seat.

"Right. Let's call the people at Health and find out what they want."

"Well, I imagine it's to do with policy."

"Perhaps."

Fenella stared at him as if he'd just declared a belief in virgin births via extraterrestrial c-section. "Or maybe they're battling a journo and want to kill the story. Let's see, shall we?"

And with that, her manicured nails reached for the phone on Martin's desk.

"Simon Tickley, please," she demanded.

"Tickley here."

The voice boomed out from Martin's speakerphone. A voice used to ordering expensive wines in central London restaurants. Martin imagined pink-cuffed shirts, silk ties and double-breasted suits buttoned up to hide a not-so-incipient beer gut.

"Simon? It's Fenella Clarke from NSO Nuneaton. I wanted clarification on your request."

"Fenella! How are you?"

Martin pictured Tickley's tongue out on a stalk, his leer echoing down the phone.

"Fine thanks, Simon."

Either Fenella was playing it very cool or she lacked any interest in dough-boy Tickley. Martin suspected the latter. "We have a new colleague – Martin Hugginson. He's going to assist me with your requests. So: do you really want multi-variant blah blah bollocks, or what's up?"

A cough at the other end. The pheasant crowed. Martin wanted to kill it, even though he'd not been in the job a week.

"Fenella, my dear. You know me too well." Tickley chuckled. "Gordon Bells on *The Times* – No-Balls Bells – uncovered our plans to offer healthcare vouchers to single mothers. He's got a hair up his arse because his wife left him and he's going to do a piece about single-father families being neglected. I need ammo for a rebuttal."

"I see." Fenella paused and looked at Martin like he was a particularly bland species of wallpaper. "Something that proves that the Southeast is full of lone daddies selflessly parenting on their own, right?"

"Right. And ask your wallah – oh sorry, Martin. Martin, if you could please prepare the full analysis to make it look proper, that would be great."

They said their goodbyes, then Fenella pressed the OFF button. She turned to Martin, her brown eyes sparkling.

Martin felt his heart turbocharge like a washing machine set to boil. Then she said, "Do you know how to do a full-stack interrogation in SQL?"

Martin shook his head. The pheasant crowed. Inwardly, he swore he'd murder it after lunch.

§

That night, Martin was eating a ready-meal curry straight out of its plastic container. He'd failed to murder the pheasant. But he had given Simon Tickley what he wanted. He'd also microwaved his meal-for-one curry for the requisite three minutes, but botched the removal of the cellophane covering such that it slopped among the sauce. He watched the TV news and navigated his mixture of cellophane and chicken Madras with a plastic fork.

The health minister came on. Martin watched him deny that healthcare vouchers were prejudicial towards single-parent families headed by men. He heard the minister talk about protecting lone fathers, who – the minister acknowledged – did a great job, constituting as many as ten per cent of all fathers in certain regions.

However, that number was complete nonsense. Martin and Fenella invented it for Simon Tickley via a statistical dump so large and impenetrable no one would read it. Least of all Simon Tickley, a policy man who didn't read at the best of times and remained untroubled by reflection of any kind. Why waste time thinking when the fate of a nation rested on your expanding paunch? The ten per cent statistic did serve one purpose, though: it launched Martin's career at the NSO.

§

Martin became adept at creating statistical reports that proved nothing. Fish stocks that weren't real. Bogus plastic card manufacturing plants somewhere near Hexham, Northumberland. Meanwhile his relationship with Fenella remained at best cool and professional; glacial might be a better word.

Perhaps his biggest thrill came from hearing the numbers he'd invented being used in newspapers, TV, and radio. OK, so he didn't invent them: rather, he drew conclusions from the evidence that weren't there because he knew that's what those asking the questions wanted to hear.

§

One day, Martin plucked up the courage to ask Fenella out for lunch on the pretence of staking out the pheasant. She accepted his invitation, even though his sexual confidence was less than zero after a three-year on-off relationship with a woman at uni who was out of his league and knew it. In other words, he'd been used – and was understandably wary. Not a good look to a young lady like Fenella.

§

"We could throw a net over it then sit on it or something. Or feed it poison seed. Or put it to sleep and drive it to Norfolk. That's kind of like dying," Martin mused as he sat with Fenella in the quadrangle, munching on a fishpaste sandwich while trying not to think about what was in said paste.

"Martin! That's shocking! How could you be so heartless to a poor, defenceless bird?"

Fenella tossed the last crust of her sandwich onto the grass and the pheasant hopped over on its one good leg to peck at the scrap of bread.

"Don't do that! You're feeding the beast!" Martin protested.

"Aren't we all, Martin? Aren't we all?"

Fenella paused then asked, "How does he stand up with just one good leg?"

Martin wondered whether he knew anything about the size of a male pheasant's wedding tackle. When he realised he didn't, he muttered something about the bird resting on his tail feathers. It was clear by this stage that his attempt to manifest an air of manly hunter-gathererness had failed.

Fenella stood up, wiped the crumbs from her packet of crisps off her dark skirt and tossed her empty Diet Coke can in the bin with a decisive thunk.

"Come on. We've got those data tables for Lincolnshire's potato production to finish."

Unable to resist such arcadian overtures, Martin screwed up his sandwich wrapper and threw it at the bin, but missed. When he went to pick up the wrapper, he thought he saw the pheasant's yellow eyes laughing as it hopped around on its one good leg.

§

Though he didn't know it, Martin's stock was rising in what might be termed the corridors of power. Those corridors were in fact a warren of offices infested with thrusting not-so-young male graduates increasingly weighed down by gut ballast and, sadly, fewer women. No one working there could have nailed two bits of wood together if their lives depended on it. Anyway, Martin's name was increasingly being spoken of in said corridors.

"Get Hugginson on it," went the cry.

Martin accompanied Fenella to the annual conference of government statisticians in London. This year, the title was "From Repository to Policy: Helping Ministers take evidence-based action". The word "repository" made Martin think of the word "suppository" – but then, he was still only twenty-two.

§

At the conference, Martin clapped loudly after Fenella's presentation and she noticed him doing so. He also met Simon Tickley in the flesh: Simon was as well-dressed and plump as Martin imagined. Tickley was also going bald, and would soon reveal aggravated indigestion caused by the over-consumption of caffeine and alcohol. In other words, he farted a lot.

In his conversation with Tickley, Martin used terms he didn't know the meaning of, such as "Pearson's R" and "Student's T," in an effort to impress. It worked – mainly because impressing Simon Tickley, a man of Olympian stupidity, was not difficult.

During the conference dinner that evening, Martin sat next to Fenella while the head of the Cabinet Office droned her way through a speech. They ate chicken Maryland made with used engine oil, or so it seemed, and drank a lot of low-quality wine. After dinner the entire conference headed for the bar at once.

Martin tagged along behind Fenella. As it turned out this was a good move. After about an hour, Fenella was visibly drunk and asked Martin to help her get back to her room.

§

Once in her room, Fenella wasted no time on preliminaries. Under the auspices of a goodnight kiss, she stuck her tongue in Martin's mouth. After a brief moment of astonishment, he responded, and before they knew where they were, as the tabloid press would say, Martin lay on Fenella's hotel-room bed with Fenella on top of him.

During proceedings he tried everything he could not to reach the top of his asymptotic curve. He thought about potato production in Lincolnshire, the number of public toilets in Cumbria, renewable energy installations off the Pentland Firth. He even thought about the pheasant in the office quadrangle, though this nearly softened his powers of analytical penetration to a catastrophic degree.

As a result of these thoughts and the amount of alcohol they had consumed, Martin managed to sustain his input until Fenella was satisfied with the results. After that she rolled over and fell asleep. Seconds later Martin was also asleep.

§

When Martin awoke, he wondered if life could get any better. His new job was going well, he had just slept with the girl of his (recent) dreams, and it seemed as if the world lay before him like an open mollusc. Only not one that lay open because it was dead.

Of course, the pheasant in the office could disappear, which would improve matters further. When he got back to the office, he no longer noticed the pheasant, though he could, admittedly, still hear it croaking.

As to Martin's self-interrogation whether life could improve further, it was about to – at least from his point of view. But perhaps not from the perspective of the British state, its taxpayers and civil servants.

§

You see, Martin began to gain power. And power, as we all know, is the greatest narcotic – or hallucinogen. For instance, Simon Tickley invited him to a shooting weekend. This consisted of people dressing up in clothes from the nineteenth century and blasting away at defenceless ducks and geese who died in agony from their wounds. Martin had never wanted to kill anything and the sight of dying birds made him feel sick. Especially if they weren't that bastard pheasant.

He went anyway because he'd been invited and thought it might be good for his career – a word he'd recently learned to attach to sitting in an office and doing what he was told to for eight hours each weekday. He also remembered the other meaning of the word "career" – to run around wildly and with no apparent purpose.

That Christmas, Simon Tickley sent him an expensive bottle of brandy from an upmarket store in London as a gift. He didn't mention that he'd put it on expenses – effectively, the taxpayer gifted Martin the brandy.

As Martin's power in government grew, so he became aware of his ability to affect change. One time he decided taxing condoms would be a great idea because he didn't like using them. So he fed the opposition parties bogus statistics about the need for better family planning. He built an argument from evidence stating that funds for this should come from the user base for family planning. The government caved in, and the world's first "Pay as you Come" legislation was born.

However much his power grew, he had still done nothing about the pheasant. He celebrated his first work anniversary over lunch in Nuneaton's most exclusive eatery. Fenella gazed at him across the table, her passion for him at its fullest flower. Amid such happiness, he remembered the pheasant back at the office and frowned.

As he perfected his own life, so the pheasant's existence became more of an affront. Soon the very idea that this bird would have the temerity to squawk and shit where he worked was offensive to him, and he swore he would remove it, come what may.

§

Shortly after this first anniversary lunch with his inamorata, Martin experienced his finest hour. After no small amount of crafty planning and inventing numbers, Martin succeeded in bringing the UK's first publicly funded Rock History Museum to Nuneaton, rather than London or Liverpool or Manchester or Glasgow or Belfast or anywhere else. He did this by supplying dodgy numbers to policy-makers too lazy or bored to check them.

He also befriended an MP who liked rock music and the sound of his own voice and made sure that said MP was properly briefed. However, the rock-music-loving MP died suddenly. He passed away true to his policy objectives, since his heart attack occurred in a hotel room in the presence of a forty-six-year-old stripper, an ounce of cocaine, a bottle of VSOP cognac and a carton of cigarettes.

His long-suffering wife was said by the media to be "devastated".

After that MP's passing, Martin's life nosedived. An independent candidate was elected to replace the rock-loving people's representative and this candidate was not just independent in name: she also possessed moral fibre, profound intelligence and a commitment to the truth. Her name was Stella Maryton and she was a single mother who believed in the free distribution of condoms.

She had short hair and her enemies spread ugly rumours about her private life. Nobody liked her very much because she was honest. Her many positive qualities meant that when she took over, she soon discovered Martin's bogus statistical evidence relating to the Rock Museum. After some further digging, she also uncovered Martin's fairy tale fish stocks, Hexham's ahistorical plastic card factory, and the filching of public funds for everything from VSOP cognac to condoms, hotels, and restaurants.

§

Meanwhile, Martin closed in on the pheasant. Not with a gun or knife or some poison food. Nor even by sticking a hungry fox or gundog in the quadrangle where it lived. No, Martin was using the deadliest weapon he knew – the power of statistics to confuse and bamboozle.

However, Martin hadn't reckoned with Stella Maryton, the advent of her anti-statistics bill, her powers of forensic research, or her capacity for networking. During the first few months of her tenure, Stella had browbeaten everyone from the cabinet secretary to the media (off the record) about how the misuse of statistics was turning the UK into a banana republic. She used the term "fantasy island", which made lots of influential people scared, because they liked to imagine both they and the country they ran mattered.

§

Based on statistical evidence, Martin constructed an argument for the legitimacy of denying existence to certain forms of wildlife (that is, killing them) on the basis of fundamental human rights such as air, water and food. Naturally this was tricky, since many would say that the wildlife had just as many rights to these things as humans.

However, by perverting a few numbers about guineafowl as carriers of various nasty pathogens, and armed with several examples of bat-to-human transmission from China which many have found useful in recent years, Martin prepared to declare numerical war on his avian adversary.

§

Stella Maryton introduced a private member's bill criminalising the use of inaccurate data to influence public policy. This was an excellent idea, since those in public life had been deluding innocent people with fake numbers for more than 3,000 years.

She gave lots of abstract and high moral arguments in favour of the bill. The kind of arguments with which everyone in public life likes to agree. Misleading stats, she argued, were divisive (true), anti-diverse (possibly, though she never explained why), racist and sexist and other things (see previous bracketed description).

The MPs loved her bill almost as much as they loved to be seen on the side of moral right. So it was passed unanimously, with just one or two old MPs who represented constituencies nobody could place on a map dissenting. The new laws were associated with a long prison term and disbarment from public life for offenders. To the MPs voting for the bill, this was the modern equivalent of being hung, drawn and quartered and having your head stuck on a pike then paraded through central London.

§

After weeks of careful plotting, Martin had the pheasant in the sights of his public policy blunderbuss. He identified some of the more venal MPs who might be persuaded to advance his anti-pheasant cause in the House of Commons in exchange for some public title – you know, those mystical letters after people's names that sound good even if you don't know what they mean.

He fed those MPs lots of statistics and charts with bullet points on them. He used terms from data science, broken up into small units so the MPs could read them out loud even if they'd had too good a lunch in a restaurant they could never afford thanks to some billionaire who wanted the government to stop taxing him.

Then Martin sat back and waited. But he was to be disappointed – majorly so.

§

The police came for Martin when he was on the phone to Simon Tickley trying to get the Department of Health to declare stray birds a health risk. They hauled him out of his chair and shoved him over his desk and tied his hands behind his back in handcuffs. Then they read him his rights and marched him off to prison in full view of Trevor the dozing nonentity and his soon-to-be-former girlfriend Fenella Clarke, who pretended not to know Martin even though her cheeks were now as red as her lipstick.

As Martin was escorted from reception by the police, he turned around and looked through the glass to the quadrangle. The pheasant was flapping around like a demented puppet. And this time he was certain: those caws, cackles, and squawks through the glass were the sounds of that deformed bird laughing at him.

A Riveting Tale

Stephan Botibol likes things just so. Consider his lunchbox: a ham sandwich wrapped in cellophane. Sufficient mustard to taste, but not to enflame the nostrils. Accompanied by a large navel orange and a chocolate cream biscuit, such is Botibol's daily lunch.

Stephan works as a welding process engineer at Penn Industries in Spalding, Lincolnshire. The company makes rivets. You know, those tiny pieces of metal that keep other pieces of metal together. There are billions of them all over the world – in aircraft, buildings, cars and machines, but almost no one knows what they are or how they work.

Stephan has seen twenty-five years of his existence evaporate during his tenure at Penn Industries. Long enough to see old man Penn replaced by his son, Sebastian "Lofty" Penn. Twenty-five years in which, every working day, Botibol has donned a pair of black trousers and sensible shirt, then driven from his red-brick home on a housing estate to Penn Industries' metal-walled workshops on an anonymous industrial estate.

If Stephan Botibol's unadventurous dress sense and constant, irrational fear of poverty betray his lower-middle-class roots, then Lofty Penn is his Polaroid negative. Lofty rolls in testosterone-soaked rides, sports designer threads and pays an attention to his diet that would shame a ballerina. He tries to come across like a lean, driven businessman since that's how he sees himself – incisive. Driven. Determined.

But Stephan's wise to the truth. Lofty knows as much about engineering as a cat does about thermodynamics – and cares less than a cat might even if it were proven that said cat knew something about thermodynamics.

Chewing on his habitual ham sandwich (see above) over lunch,

Botibol recalls the arithmetical errors he's had to correct in Lofty's technical drawings. Drawings that Lofty then passed off to clients as his own.

Well, no longer. Stephan has a new product idea, and he's sure Lofty will love it, much like some prisoners might love waterboarding, if they were mad enough.

§

Lofty Penn's Audi Turbo pulls into the Penn Industries car park. A successful entrepreneur has every right to own a vehicle like this. Not to mention it cost him less than a Porsche or Mercedes. Lofty managed to find his Audi at a police auction in Herefordshire. He'd got it cheaper than cheap – only fifty grand. In fact, Lofty praises himself, he never pays full price for anything. Including his staff.

Yes, Lofty thinks as his car doors pop open to his key fob's command, there's no fooling me. I know the value of a pound. He considers himself equally shrewd in his marriage: Melanie had far more money and far less class than him – but then, he brings intellect and his good bloodline to the conjugal bed. And he'd had no complaints so far. Well, not many.

Lofty gets out and presses his fob again. The door locks slide shut obediently. Approaching the factory, he checks his reflected fringe in the entrance door. He likes it to rest at a forty-five-degree angle to his eyebrows to hide his growing bald patch. Before opening the door he pats his taut stomach with satisfaction. Looking damn fine for forty-eight.

He opens the door and smirks at receptionist Gail. Fresh from securing a massive deal with an aircraft manufacturer to supply rivets, he feels like a six-year-old stallion in heat. Even better, that fucking nerd Botibol had just sent him some email about a revolutionary design set to make them shit-tons of cash. Whatever. As long as there's money in it. Get the patent then fire that nerd's ass before he asks for any more money.

§

Lofty hits SEND on an email telling his staff about his latest new business win, taking all the credit in an underhand way. Then that boring weirdo, Botibol, knocks on his office door and opens it. Why knock if you're going to open anyway?

Lofty has no desire to bring sandwiches to work in a plastic box like Stephan Botibol – in fact, he never eats lunch (too many calories). Also there are no sensible shirts on his back (too cheap) and no dark trousers (too boring).

He does want people to take him seriously, though. Admire him as a thinker. And that's where Stephan has it over Lofty. Stephan may be the anti-Lofty: hard-working, trustworthy and intelligent. But Lofty owns the company – and he gets what he wants. Up till now, that is.

Lofty notices Stephan clutching a brown paper bag. For a second Lofty wonders if Lord Excel Spreadsheet has brought his lunch along.

"Is that lunch, or your latest invention?"

A smile plays across Stephan's lips, thick glasses sliding down his greasy nose. His voice quivers a little:

"The latter. I hope you'll like it."

"Well, depends, doesn't it? Come on then, let's be having you—"

Stephan tips the contents of his paper bag onto Lofty's desk. More worried about possible scratches on the desk than any invention, Lofty peers at what looks like a pile of screws.

"The hell's this? A pile of screws?"

"Mr Penn, I give you – the exploding rivet!"

"The what?"

"The exploding rivet."

"What possible use is that to our customers?"

Stephan takes his glasses off, polishing them against those sensible dark trousers. Lofty glances at his email. Right now, he was leaning towards letting this bastard go on the spot.

"As an engineer, you know manufacturers employ teams of people and robots to plug rivets to bond metal sheets, right?"

"Of course I do. I have a degree in mechanical engineering, just like you."

Stephan wonders which engineering professor old man Penn had bribed to take Lofty. Or, great mystery of existence, how Lofty ever passed his exams and got a degree.

"I've invented a rivet that binds itself. You set up the two pieces of metal you need to join together. You pop these rivets in the holes.

Then you press a button on a mobile app and KERPOW!"

"Kerpow?"

"Kerpow," Stephan nods. "The rivets explode and melt, solidifying the bond between the pieces of metal. No soldering. No teams of joiners or expensive robots. Just the Penn Industries' exploding rivet – and you're done."

"Interesting."

Lofty wonders how much he can make out of this thing, and how to avoid giving Sir Botibol Borealot any more pay. After all, Lofty needs the money – the Audi is nearly three years old, too old a car for his social set. And his weekly tan and squash club membership don't come for free. In fact, maybe he could get hold of the tech drawings for this thing, then give Stephan the push. So:

"All right, Stephan. Let's chat again tomorrow, yeah? Sorry, I've got another meeting."

Lofty keeps schtum that his "meeting" is with a barber in Spalding for hair highlights. Botibol stands up and heads for the door, exploding rivets still on Lofty's desk.

"Oh, and Stephan…."

Botibol turns round.

"Take these with you. I don't want them to scratch the desk."

Botibol scoops up the rivets and Lofty notices two thin scratches in the wood. That does it – definitely no bonus, nerd boy. Not for scratching my desk. And quite possibly no job either – I'll have to pay someone to repolish the desk now.

Lofty waits until Botibol has gone, then hits a speed dial on his iPhone megapixel blahblah—

"Dennis? That you? Fancy squash and drinky-poos? Melanie's giving the kids a pizza…."

§

That night, Lofty sleeps the sleep of the just – otherwise known as the sleep of those too unencumbered with intelligence to lie awake worrying. Meanwhile, Botibol writhes wakefully in the nine-by-eleven master bedroom of his three-bed semi until he can writhe no more. He squeezes himself into his bedroom's tiny ensuite bathroom and sits on the throne to contemplate his existence.

The thing about someone like Lofty, Botibol reflects as he stares at the grime accreting under his sink thanks to years of poor cleaning, is his hereditary rights. As thick as a Lincolnshire sausage, Lofty owns Penn Industries by *primogeniture*. In other words, thank you, Daddy. It has to be said that Lofty does leaven his stupidity with some charm and a healthy dollop of greed. A combination which keeps Lofty rich – and everyone else down.

Well, no longer. I'm about to launch a remake of *Revenge of the Nerds* with more gore than *Hellraiser* – plus I'll retain the intellectual property, together with enough dough never to work again. Thus resolved, Stephan flushes the loo and pads back to bed, rolling gently onto the edge of the mattress in an effort not to wake his wife.

§

Six hours later, Stephan steadies himself before entering Lofty's office. Based on yesterday's response to his exploding rivets, Stephan is determined to ask Lofty for the partnership he'd long been promised.

"Come!" bellows a voice from within.

Hoping Lofty wasn't crying out in orgasm because he was banging someone on his desk but then secretly hoping he might be, Stephan pushes open the door.

Lofty stifles a belch as Stephan enters. Last night's squash match became a couple of beers which, in their turn, became a curry. Raghu, the owner of Lofty's favourite local Indian, finally closed the door on the two inebriated chumrades around midnight. Which means Lofty is not at his best as Botibol approaches clutching his paper bag with the screws. I mean rivets.

"Morning, Stephan. So tell me again how these things work?"

Lofty farts silently, praying it doesn't stink.

"The thing is, Sebastian, I want to discuss my partnership prospects first."

Lofty feels a little puke rising in his throat and swallows. Then he farts again, almost audibly this time. Those Indian brandies and that *kulfi* had definitely been a mistake. He's tempted to fire this fucker on the spot but can't face doing it with a hangover.

"We can talk about that later. You know I want to give you a slice of the company, only I'm waiting for further investment."

"I know. But Sebastian, you've been promising me equity for

years. I want to protect my family and my future, same as everyone else."

Lofty thinks briefly about Botibol's wife, who he once met years ago. She works in the collections department of some life insurance business in Spalding. Dull as last week's news and ugly with it. He's never met Stephan's kids, but can just imagine – choir on Wednesdays, football on Saturdays and extended bedtime on Friday nights. Already sprouting disco tits and muffin-top bellies thanks to too many oven chips and turkey twizzlers. Lower-class oiks, the lot of them.

Lofty knows he has to say something fast. He's meeting a huge aviation customer this morning and if these rivet jobbies work, he wants his first sale PDQ.

He opens a drawer and shuffles around. Underneath some photos of him and Melanie at last years' golf club dinner he finds a yellowing paper. An insurance agreement for the building. He'd never bothered to sign it, or even look at it. This'll do.

"All right, Stephan," he smiles. "Told you I was thinking about you. I'm officially making you a partner in my business. Please take your time to review these papers, then sign. Congratulations!"

Lofty stuffs the fading papers into a brown A4 envelope, slides it across his desk. He stretches out his hand for a shake, his crocodile jaw grip melting Botibol's soap-soft palm.

"I'm sorry it took me so long – I was just waiting to have a decent chat with you. Now, can we see these rivets, ffs?"

Botibol peers inside the envelope. He can't believe it – partnership at last. He stands up, gesturing towards the workshop.

"Thank you, Sebastian. Let's explode some rivets!"

"Lead on, Stephan my lad, lead on."

§

On their way down to the workshop, Stephan excuses himself and heads for the toilets. Once inside, he closes a cubicle door, sits down and opens his partnership papers. One glance and he's clued in. An unsigned insurance agreement, beneficiary name left blank. Stephan looks at the cubicle's Formica wall. WASH HANDS TO PREVENT DISEASE. Yet there was no preventing the spread of bastarditis transmitted by pricks like Lofty Penn. Once again, Lofty thought he could fob him off with bullshit. Well, not anymore.

Stephan looks at the policy again. It's worth £4,000,000. Right away, he knows how to win. How to get one over this bell-end who's been stiffing him for years.

§

Lofty Penn paces around the high-ceilinged workshop. It's 10.30, he's hungover, and their most important client is coming any minute. While waiting for Botibol to finish his dump, Lofty has visions of how he'd spend the cash from their new exploding rivets. Double the size of his house, holiday in the Jamaica sun. A yacht. How big a yacht? As big as it takes.

Maybe even a weekend nanny so the kids would bother them even less than they do being away at boarding school all week. If Botibol's gizmos work, then Lofty's lifestyle will make Bill Gates look like a tramp – and all for the price of an insurance policy that wasn't even valid.

Botibol finally comes out of the toilets, but Lofty didn't hear a flush. Lofty thinks Botibol has stress-related haemorrhoids or something.

"Listen, Sebastian. You're a busy man so I'll be brief. I'm going to set up an exploding rivets demo for this client that's coming in, OK? They'll be so impressed they'll want them right away."

Lofty prides himself on his care and attention to detail. Never lets enthusiasm get in the way of profit. But the lure of blowing his client's brain and snagging loads of money is too much.

"Sounds good, Stephan," he says. "Carry on, my man."

Botibol sets his envelope on a workbench and gets two of the guys to give him a hand. Lots of banging and movement follows, which Lofty doesn't like. So while they're working, he's in his office scrolling through GIFs of women in lingerie and worse.

Twenty minutes later, Botibol comes in to say the demonstration's ready – which is handy, because their big client has just arrived.

§

Lofty greets the clients and leads them straight to the workshop, Stephan Botibol following like a spaniel hungry for a treat.

"We want to show you our latest innovation," Lofty explains as he checks his reflection in the workshop's reinforced window, tugging at an imaginary double chin. "Our initial research suggests it removes the need for riveting in airframes. And I must credit our welding process lead, Stephan Botibol, who worked with me on this design. I'll hand over to Stephan for the demo. Let her rip!"

Ignoring Lofty's paean of pseudo-praise, Stephan taps up an app on his phone. Stephan looks at the clients in their sharp black suits and pastel ties and puts on his toniest accent.

"Welcome to Penn Industries. We've set up two metal plates with rivets inserted in the joins. Just tap the app – the rivets will explode, melt and bind the metal sheets together. Ready?"

The senior guy on the client side shuffles his feet. At the other end of the workshop, the two sheets of metal with Botibol's rivets in them hang silently in the air like judges about to pass sentence.

Botibol taps his phone. A massive bang – the roof and two walls are blown into the next county – which is Norfolk, as it happens. Dust and smoke fill the air. Lofty's clients are tossed against the wall by the blast, and Lofty himself cops a concussion.

Amid the heat and dust, Stephan Botibol grabs the insurance document Lofty tried to pass off as his partnership papers. He'd already named himself as the beneficiary and signed the document with Lofty's signature stolen from their shared drive.

Before the smoke clears, he's heading for the car park. He gets in his sensible Kia and sets off to join his sensible wife and children who wait for him at Heathrow. He'll be making a full claim against Lofty's policy from Morocco – a country that has never signed an extradition agreement with the UK. Vengeance is mine, he thinks as he turns onto the motorway. Vengeance is mine, and Lofty will pay.

By Any Other Name

"Get my nephew a publishing deal or I'll end you."

I lowered my glasses to squint at them. First, the nephew, a presumed writer. Greasy hair, thick spectacles and a downcast mouth paired with an impressive gut spilling over a pair of those skinny white jeans favoured by male models. Then the enforcer, over by the door. Andreas or Andy. A Germanic kickboxer-type: lean face, buzz-cut, leather jacket. Chewing gum like a jackhammer, leaning against the door.

That left Davy, the main man, who was talking to me. Sprawled in a chair by my desk, Davy was every gangster cliché rolled into one. Fat gold Rolex, handmade shoes and a thousand-yard stare.

"Well?"

"Well, Mr Vizziato, I can try my best—"

"No. You won't try your best. Losers try their best. My nephew wants to be a writer, y'understand? A great writer. Like Hemingway or Jackie Collins. Not some schmuck who lives in Vermont with his wife, two kids and a Volvo while he self-shills crap no one reads on Amazon and "teaches" at Buttmunch College. I'm talking balls-out, front-page-of-the-weekend-magazine, WRITER."

Outside my filthy office window the streets of Brooklyn loomed thirty floors below. My literary consultancy and agenting business was just five years old, but I'd already tasted success thanks to a couple of legitimate publishing deals plus some more lucrative ropey sidelines. Somehow I intuited Davy Vizziato's nephew would not be my next great signing.

About those sidelines I'm involved in. Some of the business I've done has been – how can I put this? – less than honest. I could tell you I was young and needed the money. The truth is I just needed the money. Like taking a cut from self-publishing companies for telling the unaccomplished that self-publishing "represents a great start". Or a cut from literary consultancies for recommending them to other hapless hopefuls who pitched me their books. It didn't make me Beelzebub – but it wasn't exactly ethical. Maybe this visit from Davy and friends was divine retribution.

But right then I was more worried about getting beaten up.

"Do you have a copy of your nephew's manuscript, Mr Vizziato?"

Davy Vizziato nodded to the nephew.

"Show him, Michael."

The nephew leaned down and scooped up a grey canvas bag. He pulled out a thick wire-bound sheaf of white printer paper, dropped it on the desk in front of me. I glanced at the title page:

MAIN STREET ARMAGEDDON
by
MICHAEL VIZZIATO

A forty-eight-point font title. Jesus. I'd only read the cover and already it looked unlovely.

"Read it."

Davy Vizziato nodded at me, eyes metastasising into toadstools of anger.

"You see, it's just that I prefer to read undisturbed—"

Davy turned to nod at Andreas / Andy the psycho. The Teutonic kill machine peeled off the wall and leapt at me. At that point – mercifully – my glasses slipped off my nose. I say mercifully, because otherwise I would have needed new glasses as well as a new set of balls.

Andreas / Andy grabbed my neck, forcing my head down against the desk. Pages from the new collection of short stories by Bamba wa Sezwe (one of my best clients: I just signed her to Random House for six figures) went flying everywhere. Andreas / Andy shoved my nose, never my most attractive feature but still the only nose I'd ever had, harder into the Formica desktop.

Davy Vizziato pulled a pistol from his waistband.

"I told you to read his book! Now read it! Read it!"

Vizziato swept all the papers off my desk and pushed the gun in my mouth. I tasted gunmetal and grease for the first time in my life. I don't think it's a combo we'll see on reputable menus any time soon. Though obviously I had more pressing thoughts. Like how to get Davy to remove his gun.

"I assure you: sign up my nephew – or your brains splat on that desk. Get me?"

I nodded that I had, indeed, comprehended his message, then flopped my head down. Andy / Andreas gave the back of my head a pitying slap and released me. I curled up pages from the manuscript by Bamba wa Sezwe between my fingers as the Vizziatos (shouldn't that be Vizziati?) left the room, their dollar-store Schwarzenegger the last to leave. He switched off the light and shut the door.

After they'd gone, I waited a few minutes, head on desk, to regain composure. Then I sat upright and fumbled, hands shaking, in my desk drawer for emergency cigarettes and brandy. Normally I'd go outside to smoke, but right then I yearned for nicotine.

I lit up with trembling fingers and tried to re-establish some order. Then I drew lustily on my cigarette, ash flailing everywhere, and picked up the nephew's manuscript. I set it down on the desk and turned to the first page:

MAIN STREET ARMAGEDDON

Prologue
Curtis Main wanted blood. And not just anyone's blood. The blood of the man who had killed his wife.

Oh pluh-lease. Revenge motive in the first line. And a Prologue? Who does "Prologues" anymore? This was already an impossible sell.

Main lit a ciguret and recalled her lithe body all over his, her tongue snakeing up his peanis just when he was about to cum

Spelling mistakes aside, of course she had a "lithe" body. And of course she fellated him. What else would any non-self-respecting, overweight teenage fantasist mistake for compelling narrative?

I looked at the cigarette between my fingers. It had nearly burned down to the filter. That I had lost track of time had less to do with Vizziato's manuscript and more to do with my panic at being maimed or killed should I refuse Davy's offer to represent his nephew.

I flipped the ash off the cigarette and took another deep draw. Then I crushed it out against the plastic cover of Michael Vizziato's manuscript, which melted and opened as willingly as the legs of a female character in what he'd convinced himself was a book.

I decided needed a sandwich. And I needed to talk to Bernie.

§

Bernie ran the deli on the ground floor of my building. He knew my order – Reuben with no mayo, lots of Dijon. Double espresso and a glass of water. That was what I always had, and today was no different. Only today I was early. And I must have looked troubled, because after he'd asked me if I wanted the usual – I nodded yes, he served it up – Bernie came over and joined me at the zinc counter next to the door. We gazed out at the street, the people bustling along.

After a while Bernie spoke, face fixed on the passers-by.

"You got problems, Josh?"

"You could say that, Bernie."

"Something to do with your visitors this morning, maybe?"

Bernie shifted his bulk in its not-so-white apron, giving me a full frontal view of those Middle Eastern features cased in thirty years of fat from tasting every lunch order before it went out.

"Uh, yeah. How'd you know?"

"I didn't like the look of them when they came in. They looked – unusual. I knew they was coming to see you. Here's my question – why'd you let them in?"

"What choice did I have? They walked into my office."

"Didn't tell you they was coming or nothing?"

"No! Of course not! One minute I'm reading someone's manuscript – the next, I'm pinned down by thugs, being told to push some garbage thriller by this guy's nephew. What would you do?"

Bernie stood up as another customer came in.

"I'll tell you what I'd do. I'd get a secretary. And a lock on my door. Good luck, kid. You're going to need it!"

§

After lunch with Bernie, I decided I would refuse to represent the great Michael Vizziato. I threw his manuscript in the garbage can, ready for the cleaners to dispatch to the fire it so richly deserved. But a phone call from Uncle Davy changed my mind.

Davy kindly repeated my licence-plate number and the make and model of my car to me, as well as my street address, cellphone number and apartment number. He told me this information, which he'd researched before our meeting that morning, would be useful to him should I choose not to represent his nephew.

He sounded in no mood to discuss further, but by the end of our little chat, I managed to get a few words in.

"I have just one question, Mr Vizziato. Why me?"

"I looked you up on the Agents Association of America website. I liked your name. That's all. That, plus the fact that I know a thing or two about some of the things you do."

I scrabbled for my cigarettes and stuck one in my mouth, then flicked my Zippo. The flame leapt up and toasted my fringe so I lowered the lighter and got the smoke going. I gazed at the manuscript in my trash can and, after a second's hesitation, fished it out with my free hand, phone clamped between my shoulder and my ear. Thank God my cleaners were late – as usual.

"Come on, Josh! Don't give me the silent treatment! I know you've been on both ends of making folks pay for publication. Wouldn't play too well with your snooty uptown buddies now, would it? Whereas a man like me, I respect your way. It's called business. Only I don't want no self-publishing, plastic-crap paper with a cover my dog could have designed. I want a top-flight publisher for my Michael. After all, he's family. And you're going to help me, Josh. That's it."

The phone went dead. So he'd looked me up on the Agents Association of America's website. He looked up a Joshua Rozenberg? There had to be a hundred Joshua Rozenbergs in the agenting business. And that was just in New York.

Quite why I'd been selected by some small-town hood to represent his nephew's trashy-trash thriller would remain a mystery. Unless, of course, I were to see it as a test by the gods. But as I was an atheist, that would be tricky. Although with what I faced right now, prayer might be a good idea....

§

I spent the weekend alternately drinking and smoking myself sick, reading parts of Vizziato's abysmal manuscript, and calling friends for advice. In order of frequency, their advice ran as follows:

1 **Call the police** – I refer you to some of my more questionable business practices. Criminal? Quite possibly, now that I come to think about it.
2 **Call a lawyer** – no good, don't have the money. And see point one above re the police.
3 **Go to the press** – I'm not well-known enough, and nothing bad has happened – yet. Also, anyone who said there's no such thing as bad publicity has never read a damning book review.
4 **Seek protection** – possible, but ruinously expensive. And I wouldn't know who to call. Even if I did, they'd probably know Davy. My mind filled with words like *omertá*, and visions of my aging mother being sent a three-day-old fish in damp newspaper. No thanks.

So in the end, I did nothing but read, drink, smoke, worry – and eat frozen microwave meals while watching bad TV. Yes, that's right: I didn't venture out of my dingy rabbit hutch in Flatbush all weekend. I'd love to tell you I had the feeling I was being watched, but the truth is I was shitting myself.

It was more than the threat of physical violence: it was also because this manuscript was so bad it worked like Ambien on my soul. Brain-rottingly bad. Not just clichéd plot or dialogue. Not just the over-boiled third-person past-tense narration, the dishwater-weak motives, the underdrawn, boring, lifeless characters, the poor grammar, spelling and punctuation: no, this manuscript was so bad it was like some malevolent force had dared me to represent this abomination under threat of death. The alternative was to invoke Davy Vizziato's anger. And no doubt I wouldn't like him when he was angry.

Monday rolled round. I hadn't slept properly for three days, not since the visit from Davy Vizziato on Friday morning. The digestion of those microwave meals had been incomplete, and I'd manage to add a world-historical hangover to my woes. Not to mention whacking my cellphone bill out of shape in my paranoid weekend of bunker-hunkering.

I had, at least, the promise of a lunch meeting with Gabrielle Shankhauser to look forward to this particular Monday.

I'd worked with Gabrielle when we both started out in publishing twenty years ago. Some dreadful digital-cum-print business on two floors of an old warehouse near the East River: the kind of place that made us feel like the struggling publishers we were. We sweated for hours while the owner of the business drove around in a Lamborghini, having lunch with his "writers" at Le Caprice. Though I turned a blind eye, the place was almost certainly a vanity publishing operation in a bikini. Anyway, it was a start for both of us.

Our careers paralleled up to the point where we both edited fiction lists for different houses. Then Gabrielle took over as MD of Toxic Books, a wildly hip, high-end publisher of literary works in translation and I sold out and became Mr Unethical Agent.

All of which meant it would be impossible for her to see my new client as a suitable prospect for her house. The author list at Toxic Books was as far distant from Michael Vizziato's, um, *style* as the Earth is from Uranus.

So after we'd sat down in a mid-range Italian joint equidistant from our respective offices, I ordered a veal cutlet while the waiter made a great show of uncorking a too-young Montepulciano D'Abruzzo. I wasted no time, broaching the subject of what to do next after as few preliminaries as possible.

I hoisted the stem of my wine glass in a toast.

"It's good to see you, Gabrielle."

She toasted me back, took a sip of her wine and set the glass down, red fingernails offsetting her strawberry blonde hair to perfection.

"Good to see you too, Josh. It's been a while. How's things?"

She was still a looker. Too much of a looker for a Jewish guy from Cleveland like me to ever have a hope. Married, two kids – but now separated, or so I heard on the grapevine. I took a sip of barely palatable wine then got down to it:

"Well, since you ask, not great. Someone says they'll kill me if I don't get their nephew a publishing deal." Gabrielle looked at me, grey eyes searching my average-to-middling-in-her-league features.

"Really? That sounds awful. Is there anything I can do?"

"I doubt it."

The waiter arrived. I realised this was the first time in four days I'd seen fresh-cooked food, so I attacked my breaded veal cutlet with gusto. Delicious – and the vegetables were perfect too. I continued devouring my steak of infant cow while Gabrielle forked at her allegedly eco-certified halibut fillet. At some point Gabrielle stopped chewing and looked over at me.

"What is it?"

She finished chewing and swallowed, then drank a little wine.

"Well…I could take that book on, if you want. Or at least I could pretend to take it on. That would get them off your back."

"Tell me more."

She put down her knife and fork and took a longer swig of her wine, unable to avoid grimacing slightly as she did so.

"Ew! This wine. Joshua, you always were a little stingy when it came to the wine list. It's why Putnam didn't appoint you to head their women's fiction list."

"Er – no. That had more to do with an unfortunate incident involving a banana and a stuffed giraffe at one of their launch parties. But let's stick to our knitting. How does this happen? I need these people off my back. I'll do anything."

"Anything? Including that new collection of stories by Bamba wa Sezwe?"

"Anything but that. You know Random House have first refusal."

"So give them something worth refusing. But let me have those stories."

I thought about it. Wa Sezwe herself had just been awarded a two-year non-teaching fellowship at Princeton. She wouldn't be too upset if Random House apparently "failed to find room" for her on their list for next spring. And I was sure I could sell Toxic Books to her as an edgier and more "street" alternative. Even if they paid less than half of what Random House offered, Princeton's munificence might make up for the rest.

"OK, OK. You have a deal. Now tell me how it works."

I got back to my veal while Gabrielle talked. As I ate, I noticed Gabrielle had stopped, knife and fork poised in mid-air. She put them down gently, took another sip of wine – less grimacing this time – and smiled.

"This is how we roll. We offer the kid a contract – not much money, though. You explain that's how it goes for first-time writers. I know you're good at that, right Josh? Don't worry, I won't mention your agreement with Primavera Publishing. You know, where you take a cut—"

"Yes, thanks Gabby. You can stop there."

"Sorry. Anyway, you tell this Michael Vizziato that's the deal. Then you give me the manuscript, and I say there have to be wholesale changes, send him off to think again for six months. Meanwhile, you leave the country on business for a few weeks – take a vacation. Things cool down while the kid is doing his rewrites. You come back, and magically you have to tell the kid we've changed our plans and his book is cancelled – no wait, better yet – postponed."

I stood up, walked round the table and bent down to kiss her cheek. I wanted to do it anyway, I was so happy – but it was a great opportunity for a schmuck like me, with my five-day beard, wire glasses and shabby linen suit, to get close to her. After we ended our hug, I straightened up and slammed into the waiter clearing up our plates. Only it wasn't the waiter. It was Davy Vizziato dressed like a waiter.

My bad: an Italian joint in Brooklyn. I should have known.

"Nice plan," Davy said. "I congratulate the pair a yous. There's just one thing."

"What's that?" Gabrielle fingered the long, thin gold pendant around her neck. Actually she twisted it like a noose, but that's just detail.

"If that book doesn't get published – and by your publishing house, lady – exactly the way my nephew wants it, you'll both pay."

Vizziato leaned over to pick up Gabrielle's half-eaten plate of halibut.

"And before you call anyone, remember: I have not threatened you. I have not harmed you. Neither of you have any proof this conversation took place."

He lifted up his waiter's apron to reveal the dull steel of a carving knife protruding from his trousers. His chunky gold watch glinted incongruously off his white shirt. "They say the *zabaglione* here is the best in the city. How about two of them, and *espresso con grappa* to finish?"

Gabrielle looked at me nonplussed. I must have looked the same, because Vizziato spoke next: "Come on! It's one little book to make my nephew happy. Whaddya say? As a favour to Davy? I knew it! Let's celebrate – dessert and coffee on the house!"

He carried the plates back across the restaurant, barking out our dessert order to a server who stood quaking in fright behind the bar. I looked across the table at Gabrielle, her usually composed face now white with fear.

"What do you think?"

Her hand reached for her half-empty glass of Montepulciano. She raised it to her lips and drained it in a swallow. She leaned back and drew in a deep breath. Then she set those steel-grey peepers on me, speaking low and hesitant:

"Please pass on my congratulations to your client and tell him we look forward to working with him."

She stood up to leave – but Davy Vizziato was back.

"Hey! Where are you going? I just brought your dessert. Siddown."

Gabby complied, bringing her chair into the table and drawing her back straight so she sat at her full height of five feet and (I estimated) eight inches.

"And while we're at it," Vizziato continued, "I brought this as well. I downloaded it off the internet and just changed the names a little."

I looked down at the sheaves of paper Viziatto placed before us. Mine was a contract for publication worth $10,000 in favour of my client. I was expected to sign for and on behalf of Michael Vizziato, author of *Main Street Armageddon*. And Gabrielle's said the same thing – for Toxic Books, and her as the publisher.

"Don't worry about the money," Vizziato said affably. "I got that – yeah, and I got your cut too, wise guy."

He slapped me on the back, then looked across at Gabrielle, face split by a melon grin. "See? This is good for everyone. I put up the money, you" – he winked at Gabrielle – "you publish the book, sweetheart – and I get to make my nephew happy. Then you get a best-seller on your hands plus a pile of dough, and you, my agent friend, you get rich too. Which is all anyone wants at the end of the day, am I right? Am I right? And neither of yous has had to do any work to get there, *capiche*? Now sign the contracts."

Gabrielle and I looked at each other across a checkered tablecloth in a cheap-ish Italian joint in Brooklyn. I toyed with my dessert spoon, the *zabaglione* melting gently on the plate in front of me. Gabrielle picked up her *espresso con grappa*, her gorgeous lips sucking in that potent brew like a snake licking water. I picked mine up and did the same.

"*Salute*," offered Davy Vizziato. "Now sign the contract."

"Er, Mr Vizziato. I think we should have a discussion about the literary merits of your nephew's wor—"

"I said sign the contract, my Roseybloom friend. Before things get messy, get me?"

Vizziato produced a high-end black fountain pen from his pocket and handed it to Gabrielle, who scrawled her signature on the last page, then looked away in disgust.

"Wait a second, wait a second," muttered Vizziato. "You need to acknowledge your rights and duties as a publisher. Your initials on pages three and nine, please."

Gabrielle scribbled briefly on both pages as required.

"Thank you. Now it's your turn, Mr Rozenberg." I did what I had to do, my heart sinking as my hand moved across the page.

"But Mr Vizziato. What about the literary merits of—"

"Literary merits my ass. You think Shakespeare had any literary merit? No! The sucker had the king's dough behind him. That's how the world works!"

"The queen," I mumbled.

"Excuse me?" Viziatto glowered at me and reached for his belt. Right where he'd packed that knife.

"There was a queen, not a king, on the throne most of the time Shakespeare was writing. Although admittedly a king showed up later on...."

"Listen kid. You'll learn two things working with me. Never get technical. And never get fresh. You got that?"

I nodded and looked across the table. Quiet panic suffused Gabrielle's face. Her hands gripped the table edges.

"So like I said. I'm the king. I got the dough. And yous two is gonna put my dough and your pull behind my nephew. And before long, he'll be on the cover of the *New York Times Magazine*. Just like a real writer."

"But Mr Vizziato, I insist—"

OK, I'll admit it. I was probably trying to impress the newly separated Gabrielle. Big mistake.

Vizziato grabbed me by my lapels and pushed me down into my chair. He leaned in so close I smelled the garlic sweat and stale cologne.

"No, my skinny friend. You don't insist nothing. Not if you know what's good for you." Then he shoved me to the floor. "Sir! I'm so sorry, sir! But hey, maybe sir shouldn't drink red wine and grappa together, sir!" he said loudly, drawing the attention of the other diners. He helped me back into my seat, then gathered up the contracts from our table.

"Thank you very much, lady and gentleman. This meal is on the house. Our lawyers will review these contracts and get you copies by close of business tomorrow. Pleasure doing business with you."

Vizziato took up our empty cups and glasses, turning towards the bar. My eyes following him, I spotted the pudgy nephew-cum-writer at the bar drinking a beer, and Andreas the enforcer polishing a glass with ostentatious care behind the bar, his hulking body obscuring the colourful rows of bottles on back-lit shelves. I turned back to the table – but Gabby had vanished.

§

The next three months passed in trying to convince Michael Vizziato he wasn't ready for publication. Would he reconsider the character of Curtis Main? He would not. Might he think again about a plot that involved more minor characters than the crowd at a Yankees game? Nope. To make matters doubly difficult, these writerly refusals were delivered through the intermediary of Davy Vizziato – with Andy / Andreas providing muscular persuasive force for Davy at each rendezvous.

Once every two weeks I met them on the sidewalk outside a basketball court near Brooklyn's toughest school. Never mind my two hoodlum acquaintances – I feared for my life every time I walked past that place. The smell of chronic wafting through the air, over-muscled, under-educated teenagers shooting hoops in sleeveless T-shirts and Tupac head-scarves….

Vizziato turned up in a different ride every time. One time a Volvo SUV that had seen too many salt-roaded winters. Or an old Dodge van. All beat-up jalopies on their last legs – conspicuously inconspicuous, if you will. I'd be ushered into the back next to Davy. Andreas would sit up front at the wheel. There'd be a weapon of some kind poorly hidden in either the seat pocket in front of Davy or resting on the passenger seat next to Andreas / Andy.

Then I'd give my update on how things were going. Explain the process – editing ("not too much. I don't want you taking away my nephew's meaning or nothing"), typesetting ("just put the goddam words on the page. How hard can it be?"), and, finally, the thorny questions of cover art and supporting quotations from other writers. And all that before we got on to the sales and marketing plan.

Unsurprisingly, I'd made a tacit agreement with Gabrielle that we wouldn't be approaching any established writers for comment on *Main Street Armageddon*. In fact, if we could get away with it, we wouldn't be marketing the book at all. We'd let Davy Vizziato pick the venue for the launch party, invite their hoodlum buddies and family, have them buy books over cans of Pabst Blue Ribbon or whatever it was these people drank, and that would be it. Job done and we could all move on.

Except Davy had been doing research – again. Of course he had.

At our next meeting, Davy and Andy / Andreas showed up in a red and tan 1977 Ford Pinto. The last model to be built before they were banned for the explosive tendencies of their gas tanks. Davy leaned over and wound the window down.

"Get in," he said.

He styled a 1980s heavy-metal T-shirt, while up in front Andreas / Andy looked like something out of a '90s dance video, white plastic shades, skinny pink T-shirt with BLACK ARMS MATTER on it and red leather pants. Despite the uber-gay dancehall gear, he still looked like he'd kill you easy as picking his nose.

"You got that thing you owe me?"

That phrase alone convinced me I was no longer just the enforced literary agent for Davy's nephew. Davy addressing me in the language of the *famiglia* told me I was on the inside now.

I nodded and handed over the uncorrected proofs of his nephew's magnum opus, bound in thin scarlet cardboard with the words UNCORRECTED PROOF COPY FROM TOXIC BOOKS in thick black letters on the cover. Any young hipster would be showing that off on the subway as a sign of literary credibility. But to me, it was like a vial of bubonic plague.

"Good…that's good. I like that."

He threw the proof on the front seat. It landed with a thwack on top of a crowbar which Andy / Andreas had left lying there to encourage me.

"Hey, Andy!" Davy said to his henchman. "Our little buddy here is gonna make my nephew a star!" Davy put his arm around my shoulder.

"You done good, kid. We'se all proud of you. Now, Andy and me are going to take you to another meet with the author, Michael."

Vizziato spoke those words in the tone I imagine one might use with a new writer about to commune with the spirit of the late Cormac McCarthy at a seance.

"You see, we've been researching book promotion. I reckon we'll be able to show you a thing or two. Andy – hit it. We gotta be in the East Village asap."

Andreas fired up the Pinto, releasing the handbrake and crunching through second and third of that ancient banger, tyres pleading for mercy as he did a 180 and headed for the Brooklyn Bridge.

§

When we reached the bar where we were supposed to meet nephew Michael, I realised why Andy and Davy had dressed like '90s clubbers. They wanted to fit in and not be noticed. So they wore clothes a middle-aged mobster thought hipsters would wear.

The results were disastrous. Instead of blending in, they stood out among all the beards and tweeds worn by men twenty-five years younger than them. At best, they looked like married businessmen trying to cop younger women: but they were just badly disguised hoods on the make.

Michael Vizziato, great author-in-waiting, sat at a long, low table, the remnants of a piece of chocolate cake and a half-finished latte in front of him. He wore tiny smears of chocolate around his lips, his glasses half an inch down his nose. It was warm in here – maybe that made people drink more. Or eat more, or something. Either way, it didn't look like Vizziato Junior had a problem with either eating or drinking.

Davy embraced Michael and Andreas / Andy gave the chubby youngster a brief nod. The two men sat down either side of me, and Davy pulled a pocket notebook out of his leather jacket.

"Now let's see…I got the email address of James Wood at the *New Yorker*. I mean his gmail address, not the one monitored by his assistant at Harvard. I also got Amy Bloom at the *New York Times*. For endorsements, I was thinking maybe Wole Soyinka? And that Japanese guy, whassisname, you know—"

I hazarded a guess.

"Haruki Murakami?"

"Yeah, yeah, that's it. I got his Skype details in Tokyo. I just didn't know how to say his name."

"Wait a minute—"

Vizziato fixed me with that worrying stare. Andreas looked at his boss, all set to hurt me on Davy's command.

"What is it, Joshua?"

"How did you get James Wood's personal email? And Murakami's Skype? These things are gold dust."

"Listen to me. Don't worry about it. I'll take care of everything, Joshua. All you need to do is call these people, get them to say nice words for the back cover. That's all I'm asking for. Come on, please. As a favour to Davy. You know."

I stared into some unseen void before me. As an adult with what I considered an average level of self-esteem and a decent if slightly shady career, I sensed I was getting out of my depth. Calling James Wood and asking him to endorse a pile-of-crap thriller we had no intention of publishing was not high on my list for career enhancement. Nonetheless, I knew lying was my only way out of this situation with my spleen and reputation intact. So: "OK. I'll do it."

"Attaboy! You want a drink or something? Steady your nerves a little?"

"Double brandy," I answered. "Martell XO. Straight up."

Davy clicked his fingers in the direction of the bar while Andreas relaxed into the thick-stuffed dark leather sofa. On the other side of the table, Michael the plump nephew smiled and pushed his glasses back up his greasy nose.

"It's nice to spend some time with my agent at last," he offered, then took another pull on his latte before scraping the chocolate cake plate with his fork for the last few crumbs.

"Hey Michael," Davy grinned. "Let me do the talking, aaite? You're the writer. Real writers don't use too many words. Get me?"

My brandy arrived, along with espressos for Andy / Andreas and Davy and a thick hot chocolate topped with cream for Michael. Davy handed me my drink, then gave the waiter a rolled-up hundred-dollar bill before passing Michael his hot chocolate with a look of unvarnished disgust.

"Here's to my nephew's success as a famous writer," said Davy, holding up his cup in mock salute. "And to him losing forty pounds and finding a girlfriend at last."

Andreas / Andy and Davy laughed up a riot. Michael scowled and put down his drink with a thunk. I downed my brandy in a single snort and called for another. I needed to get out of here fast – if not physically, then at least by getting wasted.

§

The passage of two hours found me three-quarters drunk, listing like some pissed trawler behind my desk back in the office. Yes, the same desk Vizziato almost flattened my nose into a few months ago. I might be forced to agent for them, but I wasn't about to accept their decorating advice.

Sozzled as I was, I now faced the prospect of Skyping one of the world's most famous novelists out of the blue, asking him to blurb some un-thrilling thriller. Likewise, I was supposed to call James Wood, the English-speaking world's greatest living critic, and ask him to sully his reputation – to say nothing of his eternal soul – by effusing over this garbage. And I was smashed at 3.30 on a rainy Tuesday in Brooklyn. So I did what any normal man would do in the circumstances: nothing.

I toyed with my phone for a while, pushing it in and out of its cradle to hear the comforting bleep as it slipped back into charging mode. I thought about having a cigarette, but read a few pages of the Bamba wa Sezwe manuscript instead.

When I saw the clock on my wall had crawled past four p.m., I decided I could plausibly call Gabrielle and update her. And maybe get her out for a drink as well. I called her office phone and she picked up after one ring.

"Josh. We need to talk."

"I was just thinking the same. I've, well, I've been reconsidering things."

"So have I. And probably not in the same way as you. Drinks this evening. In fact, Josh, just get here now."

Twenty minutes later I was leaning against the bar of some joint called 20/20 a couple of blocks from her office with a bourbon on ice, waiting for her to show. Two minutes after that, she breezed in, air-kissing me perfunctorily.

I smelled some expensive English perfume off her, roses and peonies. It only made me want her more. I'm not sure the reek of too much liquor made her feel the same way about me.

"I don't know if I can go through with this," she said after ordering a glass of white considerably superior to the red I'd ordered back in that Brooklyn trattoria.

"I know what you mean. But if we don't go through with it, he'll kill us. Or worse, cripple and disfigure us. Well, disfigure you. With this nose, maybe I could use a little disfigurement."

Her wine arrived. Ignoring my efforts to generate sympathy through self-deprecation, she thanked the waiter then cradled her glass in her hands.

"You know, there might be another way."

"I'm listening."

She brushed a strawberry hair strand away from her eyes.

"We could go full irony. Get the proofs in the hands of critics right now. Explain that Vizziato and Toxic Books are offering a hyper-real critique on masculinity and the conventions of the thriller with this groundbreaking work."

"Uh...."

"I know. They won't buy it. But who cares? It'll get us off the hook with Vizziato. Then we can go back to normality. Listen, everyone's allowed one bum book in their careers, right? I mean, look at Saul Bellow—"

"I'm not too sure our friend Michael fits in the same category as the Jewish Dickens," I offered.

Gabby took a swallow of wine and set the glass down, fingers running up and down its stem. Then she looked up.

"Joshua, do you ever get lonely?" My back stiffened, then other parts decided that was a good idea and followed suit. I gave a non-committal shrug. She paused, then tried a more obvious tack.

"I suppose what I'm really trying to say is…"

…and she leaned across and whispered something. I stood up and took her hand without another word, motioning for the check. Then I reached for my cellphone, trying to hit up the Uber app. I couldn't get us home soon enough.

§

Afterwards, we lay together on my scuzzy mattress for a long time, talking. She gathered the thin sheets around her toned body, the same sheets I'd been meaning to wash for the past ten days, and lay back into my pillows with a sigh. Not much about my apartment was up to standard, but I'd always insisted on good pillows.

"Mmmm…."

"What?"

"That was my first time."

I stared at her, thinking for a moment she was trying to claim her entire thirteen-year marriage had been an unconsummated, arid sham and that she was saving herself, like a coy teenager, for the acme of male perfection I so obviously represented. I decided to seek clarification.

"You mean, the first time since you left your husband?"

She nodded dreamily. So I guess that settled any debate about my perfection. I scrabbled for the pack of cigarettes on the other side of my bed. Maybe the hiatus from sexual activity on her side explained why, after a long time spent with the usual preliminaries, she'd dug her fingernails into my chest and screamed so loudly I thought the windows might shatter.

In a metaphor stolen from the pages of Michael Vizziato's

manuscript, I followed her up the slopes of ecstasy, then we lay there saying nothing awhile. Eventually, after using the image of Michael Vizziato to curb any fresh awakenings, I took out a cigarette and lit up, inhaling deeply.

"Oh, Joshua. You're going to have to quit smoking indoors. I can't stand the smell."

I took another drag then stubbed out my smoke against a speculative submission I'd been sent from some creative writing MFA newly graduated from Boston College.

"…and we've got to find some way of getting this gangster off our backs."

I nodded and leaned in to kiss her – but my phone rang. Eyes still on her epic form, I reached across her to pick it up.

"Yo Josh. How's that marketing plan? You talk to Jimmy Wood or that Jap guy yet?"

I looked at Gabrielle. She turned away to look at the far wall, cigarette smoke from my stubbed-out butt raftering up under the bedside light on my side.

"Oh, Davy. I was just discussing our plans with Gabrielle from Toxic Books."

"Discussing. Is that what yous call it now? I'm down below your apartment on the street. In my car. My real car – the Maserati. Not some Pinto shit. Listen – we need action, kiddo. You're publishing in six weeks. I want a list of who got the proofs. Who's getting invited to the launch party. And I want" – Gabrielle pulled her legs out from under mine and headed to the bathroom – "I want the distribution plan and sales incentives worked up by your hot little friend from Toxic Books."

I glanced nervously over to my bathroom, hoping Gabrielle wouldn't find the old copies of *Maxim* or, God help us, *Men's Health*, I'd left in a pile next to the toilet.

"Yes, Davy. Yes, you're right. I'll make sure Gabrielle gets you that stuff. Right away."

"Good. See? I told you I knew a thing or two about publishing. It's easy. I don't know why you people got to moan and jaw all the time. You watch, boy. We're gonna be rich!"

I put the phone back in its cradle. Gabrielle wouldn't be pleased.

I turned round and there she was, naked in the doorway between bathroom and bedroom. She held a copy of *Men's Health* at her torso, making no attempt to hide her glories above and below the fold, as it were.

"Joshua. No self-respecting heterosexual reads this magazine. Is there something you want to tell me?"

Oh, I had lots to tell her all right. And none of it was good.

§

Six weeks later, launch day came like some evil curse. Davy had chosen the Italian place in Brooklyn for the launch. Yep, the same eatery where I'd got Gabrielle into all this mess. Where he'd given me a little taster of what awaited if I challenged him.

I'm happy to say Gabby and I had blossomed into an item over the last month despite my reservations that she might have been – in fact, probably still was – on the rebound from her ex-husband. And out of my league anyway.

A few weeks ago she'd introduced me to her kids whom she had during the week. And I'd stayed over at her place a couple of times at weekends. It was all bubbling along nicely. But my relationship with Gabby was about the only good thing at that moment.

The whole run-up to the launch had been by some distance the strangest experience of my professional life. Actually, my entire life. As you maybe guessed, we didn't push too hard on James Wood or *The New York Times* for a review. Yet such was the pulling power and reputation of a hot press like Toxic Books that we got reviews for *Main Street Armageddon*, all right, even if we didn't want them.

Let's say none of them were overly positive. Indeed, they were among the worst reviews I'd ever seen:

Inexplicably, Toxic Books have chosen to publish a thriller that redefines puerile fantasy. Dragged down by one-dimensional characters, a ludicrous plot and sentences constructed from Jell-O, Michael Vizziato's *Main Street Armageddon* is the literary equivalent of watching a multi-car pileup. One reads in fascinated horror, amazed by how much worse it can get – and it does....

—Publishers Weekly

Hip young outfit Toxic Books, which recently spirited trendy Zimbabwean novelist Bamba wa Sezwe away from Random House, has blotted its copy-book with this stinker. Not even so bad it's good – just bad, period.

—Kirkus Reviews

And so on. You will be unsurprised to learn I did not quit smoking or drinking as these reviews came through. In fact, I got so stressed Gabrielle and I plotted more than once to leave the country with her kids, fearing what Vizziato and Andreas might do to us if they saw them. But Davy and Andy don't read. That's not their forte. Muscle is their forte.

Much the same could be said of the crowd at the launch party. I suspected the last time anyone there apart from Gabby and I had read a book was a Yellow Pages ad for pizza in the '80s.

To get the launch started, nephew Michael read one of his scrotum-tighteningly bad sex scenes. He followed this with around 400 words of graphic violence that constituted the book's *dénouement* (neither Gabby nor I had ever read the thing all the way through – we'd cracked, and paid a freelancer for the copy-edit).

After Michael finished reading, cue loud applause, whoops, air-punching and other noises more appropriate to sports stadium bleachers than a book launch. Michael Vizziato hauled his bulk over to a cheap wooden table next to the microphone and sat down in front of copies of *Main Street Armageddon*, its garish black-and-yellow cover glinting in the spotlights Davy had encouraged (forced) the restaurant to install for the launch.

Vizziato relatives and business associates duly formed a long line for Michael's signature in his tome. After he'd signed, each silently handed a twenty-dollar bill (though I saw a few fifties as well) to Donna, Gabrielle's publishing associate at Toxic Books, who stood by the table collecting cash like an undertaker accepting regrets on behalf of the family.

An hour later it was all over. Although the Vizziatos and their associates dug in hard on the food and drink paid for by Davy, the snack tables still groaned with uneaten *bruscetti*. I also noticed a few open, but undrunk, bottles of a fetching Valpolicella Ripasso. I had a mind to relieve Davy of those – provided I could get him to look the other way.

At that moment he was counting up the money earned at the launch. He squared the wads of bills expertly once Donna finished counting each one, tucking each stack away in a cheap black briefcase. I took a step towards the overloaded food and drinks table.

I'd planned to swipe the Valpolicella on a pretext of joining Gabby outside where she was having a smoke. But Davy's criminal radar must have been set to stun, because he turned round after I'd taken my first pace towards that luscious booze:

"Hey yo! Josh! Check it out! Three thousand six hundred dollars of sales. And that's just the launch. Wait till word gets around. C'mere…" – and with that, Vizziato beckoned me over.

I crossed the restaurant dumbly, hoping Gabby would get back from her cigarette soon. Vizziato put an arm around my back and patted me on my linen-clad shoulder.

"Y'see, kid? They say the pen is mightier than the sword. But I'll tell you what" – and here he leaned in so I could smell the Old Spice cologne, see the butt of a pistol in his coat pocket – "a gun ain't too bad neither. Hey! I just made up a poem! Wanna hear it?"

I nodded miserably, stomach tightening into some strange Gordian knot.

"They say all men are created equal
But put me behind the trigger – and I'll write a different sequel."

"Ya like that, kid? Huh?" He smiled and put a roll of bills in the top pocket of my sports jacket. "There you go, my friend. Take that lady of yours out tonight and celebrate."

Then he kissed my cheek, giving it a vice-like pinch. I nodded by way of thanks and staggered off to find Gabrielle. We were going to celebrate all right. Celebrate our freedom. Celebrate being released from Davy Vizziato's brooding threats of violence and Michael Vizziato's abysmal prose. And celebrate our relationship. Our return to professional normality.

§

There are times in life when we think we know the answers in advance. And that's when life usually proves us wrong. Almost always, in my experience, on the downside. But not every time.

So you probably think Michael Vizziato's novel was an epic failure after those reviews. After it was so poor. Am I right? Well, the news is – no. In fact, it ended up as one of the year's best-selling thrillers. I mean, not James Patterson, or anything, but still. It became by some distance the best-selling book Toxic had ever published.

In literary circles, the novel excited debate between those who (correctly) believed it to be unpublishable dreck, and those who thought it a brave and ironic *cri de coeur* on the part of disaffected masculine youth. And then – need I add – there were those disaffected masculine youths themselves, aged thirteen or so, with parents desperate for them to spend less time on screens and more between the covers of a book.

Michael Vizziato's tales of misogynistic sex, absurd violence and wish-fulfilment immoral heroics fitted early teenage tastes and *Weltanschauung* perfectly. The book erupted on Amazon. Within six months we'd had an offer from Scribner to free him from our first refusal rights. An offer of US$100,000, which we duly accepted.

For the first time in my life, I had some spare cash. Eighteen months after that, Scribner published Vizziato's second novel, *The Gods in Heat*. At this point, things took a turn into an alternative universe. Desperate to widen its appeal beyond academia and bored media executives, the *New York Review of Books* decided to invite Michael Vizziato to give them his "books of the year".

Because Michael hadn't read any more books than his career-criminal uncle, he turned to me for advice. Alongside a couple of tactical, log-rolling plugs for clients and friends, I foolishly gave him two really interesting choices by little-known, oh-so-hip writers.

And thus the myth of Michael Vizziato as literary *cognoscente* was born. The book world decided Viziatto's first novel, *Main Street Armageddon*, had indeed been a brilliant literary *trompe l'oeil* birthed by a superior intellect. So it was that in one of their editions published in the following spring, London's *Times Literary Supplement* carried a full-page article by Michael Vizziato on "The Hero as Unreliable Narrator" in popular fiction.

I could only wonder which unfortunate post-graduate teaching assistant Davy had strong-armed into writing that, because it wasn't half-bad. And that article, in turn, led to a couple of appearances on some European late-night discussion programmes where cultural rent-a-mouths opine upon the challenges of economic development in post-colonial Africa in fifteen seconds or whatever.

Just showing his face on such TV shows – on PBS, Britain's Channel 4 and even (with the aid of a translator, *naturellement*) France's *Arte* was enough. Michael Vizziato was – if not canonised – then at least declared among the blessed of today's literary elite.

§

Passing through JFK on the way to an agent's conference in Austin just after Viziatto's sophomore work was published, I found myself unable to resist taking a look at the display stand in Barnes and Noble for my enforced protégé's new offering. A black cover, of course, with the name MICHAEL VIZZIATO in giant embossed silver letters, rising out of the stygian darkness like car headlights during a drive-by shooting.

On the back cover, quotations from the introductions European Art-TV presenters gave him, complete with one of those half-on, knowing-grimace black-and-white headshots that airbrushed half his fat away and minimised the deleterious effects of his pudding-bowl haircut.

I opened the book. After the title page came this dedication:

For Joshua Rozenberg and Gabrielle Shankhauser, who first recognised my gifts.

So there it was. A happy ending? Not really. Some talentless schmuck just got a big publishing deal by using foul means and intimidation, sending the wrong message to tens of thousands of struggling writers who would assume Michael Vizziato's schlock was what publishers really wanted.

But maybe the whole story had a successful outcome. Certainly for Gabby and me – we found love. And Uncle Davy got his nephew the writerly fame he'd promised.

As for Michael Vizziato himself, I wondered how he would look back on all this in ten or fifteen years' time, when he'd (hopefully) grown enough as a human being to see what he'd written for the dross it was. Or maybe he'd think it a success, because he'd been published and made money.

In the end, whatever you called it, the whole thing proved educational. Not least it taught me that reading should be about pleasure, even for the frustrated teenage boys buying Vizziato's books, and not about duty.

Who cares what labels critics and editors put on books? It's in the reading that we know them. And each of us comes to know a book in our own way. After all, to borrow words from someone the Vizziatos would probably never read, "A rose by any other name would smell as sweet."

My Grandmother's Russian Doll

You've probably heard of people like Granny Mary: the sort of person who uses a Roman legionnaire's shield (a real one, 2,000 years old) as a door-stopper. Who has a pack of Irish wolfhounds meandering around a pebble-dashed bungalow in Cork from which she watches the years pass while soaking in sentimental recollection, cheap sherry and cheaper cigarettes.

Now – after consuming more ethanol and nicotine than an oil rigger for over seventy years – Granny Mary has passed to her maker at ninety-three years young. Our family thus descended on her estate like flies on the proverbial: myself, my sister Charlotte and my brother's widow Nadyezha. We are all nakedly after her money, as well as anything else worth having.

Being the grandchildren of wealth, Charlotte and I were not well-disposed to a career – after all, our parents hadn't been, though we at least managed to outlive Granny. Mummy and Daddy spent all forty-eight years of their marriage waiting for Grandma to die, but to no avail.

While anticipating Grandmama's demise, I'd been obliged to take an occupation. In my youth, I'd tried many jobs: film production, writing, anything. In the end, I settled to earning a competence from insurance broking. A job by no means commensurate with my tastes, but it gave me something to talk about at parties.

Granny's will divided the paintings, crystal *et cetera* between myself, Charlotte and Nadyezha. But the will made no mention of the aforementioned Roman door-stopper (I mean shield), or a set of *matryoshky* – Russian dolls, allegedly fashioned by the House of Fabergé in the last years of the Romanoff Tsars.

Oxford's Ashmolean Museum expressed an interest in the Roman shield for £60,000. As this enabled us to calm our debts, we accepted with alacrity – which left the aforementioned dolls. Being Kazakh (not quite Russian, but let's not split heirs, haha), Nadyezha said she knew people in Moscow who could sell them for £10,000,000. The thing is, neither Charlotte nor I trust Nadyezha to give us the right time of day – far less manage the sale of what's rightfully ours.

§

No one knew where Granny got those dolls: it had never arisen in conversation. Typically, one would feed Granny's noxious stews or *vel sim* to the wolfhounds, only to discover them shitting out said repast on the lawn less than two hours later. You usually became so drunk – both at Granny's encouragement, and by choice – that discussion proved impossible.

The drunkenness of our visits explains why we never noticed the dolls, which looked like large dust balls when we cleaned out her house. However, assiduous cloth-wiping revealed ten dolls exquisitely painted in red and goldleaf, each hidden inside the next, the hatbands on their matronly outlines studded with diamonds and emeralds. The initials "CF" were painted on their base in Cyrillic, together with the year MDCCCXCVII – 1897.

"Is Fabergé doll. I sure. Looks like Fabergé egg, only doll."

Nadyezha had many talents, especially in the bedroom – or so my late brother assured me – but I suspect the valuation of antiques was not among them. She claimed to be thirty years younger than Peter, though she may have lost a few years somewhere. Now about thirty-five, she wore her straw-coloured hair in a ponytail and painted her nails in an on-trend rainbow.

"How can you be sure it's not a trinket?"

My sister Charlotte – similarly unqualified to comment, and decidedly less glamorous than Nadyezha. A gambling habit coupled with our genetic lack of ambition fitted her for little in this life. In her early sixties and greying fast, she was a caring person, though this care was usually directed to dogs and horses who could not disappoint her with their opinions.

"Perhaps we ought to get it properly valued," I suggested.

"Is bad idea. Valuator lie, then take big commission. Let Russian sell doll to Russian."

I looked across at Charlotte, who gave one of those little shrugs I'd come to know so well. A shrug that combined sarcasm with *m'enfoutisme* in the face of fate. The same shrug she'd given when Peter announced he would marry Nadyezha after lifelong bachelordom.

Peter encountered Nadyezha on a jaunt to meet the panjandrums of Kazakhstan's petroleum sector in his role as chief PR wallah for an oil company. She was a PA, but after meeting Peter she gave up her job to concentrate on cleaning him out of his savings. There ensued a brief interlude sailing round the world in a thirty-nine-foot yacht which ended when he crashed into a Japanese freighter in the English Channel shortly after launch. Circumnavigating the globe thus became two blissful months of fornication in a *gîte* somewhere in the less frequentable parts of Normandy.

However, I digress. The process of valuing our dolls was soon to change our plans – indeed, life quickly became not so much surreal as completely absurd.

§

"It's an amusing little thing – and the jewels are real – but Fabergé had no hand in them."

I stared across the walnut desk at my interlocutor, a man rejoicing in the name of Reginald Duck. Auctioneer, valuator and "specie risk consultant", whatever that means. Charlotte and Nadyezha sat either side of me as point and counterpoint to my *haut-bourgeois* respectability.

"Not!" countered Nadyezha. "Is Fabergé. I sure. How much worth, anyway?"

Mr Duck peered at her over rimless spectacles, unused to such challenges to his authority. I wore the only suit I owned, cut by Hawkes of Saville Row rather longer ago than I or my waistline cared to remember. I complemented this with my old Malvernian tie just to show I wasn't an oik. Charlotte added to my respectability with her demure rollneck, our mother's pearls and a tweed skirt.

"Not more than £200,000. Top whack." Mr Duck's fairground huckster side was showing. "Many jewellers set themselves up as alternatives to Fabergé in the late imperial period: the lawsuits and counter-suits surrounding such obfuscations were interesting. That is, until your country's history was, er, somewhat truncated by events."

"What truncate? I truncate you. Give me doll. I get valuation from Russian which knows what they talk in."

Nadyezha showed enough of her impressive *décolletage* to distract Mr Duck from our dolls. Nadyezha's attire reminded me of when I first met her. "I know you think I am dig gold. But I love Pete," she said simply. And perhaps she did – but she also loved money. And glittery objects. Lots of them.

After we left Mr Duck, Nadyezha launched a series of Zoom calls to the motherland. Forty-eight hours later the three of us were clustered around Nadyezha's laptop, peering into the gloomy office of one Sergei Malenkoff, "valuation expert for greater Russia".

I noticed from the little back-reflector camera in her phone that Nadyezha and her mammaries took up half the screen and the dolls most of the rest. In consequence, Charlotte and I were reduced to supporting presences, like human bra straps, while Malenkoff inspected the doll via webcam link. After a lengthy conversation in Russian punctuated with lots of "Da"s, Mr Malenkoff began in stilted English:

"No doubt is Fabergé. Not known for *matryoshky*, but did them still. Price is $10,000,000 in Russia."

I glanced at Charlotte. $10,000,000 – £2,000,000 each, give or take. Sufficient to allow me to spend freely until I expired, and even leave a few shekels to David and Judy – our children who had, to date, carried on the family tradition of insouciant idleness with aplomb.

Might I offer some of my share to charity? I might, depending on how much remained after I'd paid off my debts and looked after my children. After allowing Nadyezha to blither on in Russian for a bit, I interjected, acting like the kind of Englishman who believes the Empire has yet to crumble completely:

"Now look here. I trust all three of us may attend this auction?"

"Naturally," said Malenkoff, hands making an expansive gesture. "I look forward to welcome you motherland with Nad'ya!"

Moscow, here we come. Land of Pushkin, Stravinsky, and more

criminal activity per square mile than anywhere else on earth.

§

In what seems, looking back, to have been an act of outrageous optimism, the three of us booked the Baltschug Kempinski, one of Moscow's finest and most expensive hotels. Naturally, we'd done so at Nadyezha's suggestion:

"Is only proper place for lady, like I am will be, to stay."

Sale day arrived, and found Nadyezha locked in our suite's main bathroom, potioning and bathing and whatnot. Charlotte sat on the edge of her bed, nervously sipping a cup of English breakfast from a white Minton cup. I paced about the carpet, worrying.

Who in hell would pay 10,000,000 for these things? How would we get the money home? And how to avoid world-historical sums of tax?

I cannot lie – I also harboured thoughts of delicious idleness. If I lived as long as Granny, I might enjoy thirty more years of loafing, exquisite wine and listening to opera. I pictured myself strolling country lanes in the Welsh borders, knocking heads off thistles with a stick and feasting on gastropub lamb and treacle tart while getting squiffy on the local ales.

Finally Nadyezha surfaced from her *toilette*. Her hair, normally left hanging to her shoulders, was pinned up in a loose bun. She'd paired a white blouse with black slacks and tan cycling pumps. I wore my suit from Hawkes, and Charlotte, a smart navy dress, again with mother's pearls.

A cab, haphazardly driven by a wall-eyed Uzbek who stank of stale beer and piss, and more of the latter than the former, delivered us to the auction house in good time for the start of proceedings at six p.m. This was the hour when, we were assured, Russia's wealthiest businessmen and their wives would have a little time to spend before dinner at some chic restaurant in the Arbat district.

The auction house itself appeared suitably grand: oak-panelled entrance, brass railings and an embossed nameplate in Latin and Cyrillic lettering. A pretty young thing in a business suit welcomed us at the door with excellent English, then showed us through to the auction hall. Our dolls were the third lot for sale, with the reserve price set at $2,000,000 – low enough, we were told, to attract interest yet high enough to assure prospective buyers of their quality. The catalogue described our *matryoshki* (in Russian, English and what I assumed was Chinese) as "authenticated by Professor Sodanyoff, former head of the Khlestakov Art Institute".

The room began to fill up. We were placed at the back to ensure we remained inconspicuous. Though not inconspicuous enough, as things transpired.

§

Just before kick-off, a young man in a navy suit approached us and spoke to Nadyezha in Russian. She replied, looking first at me then Charlotte. She seemed to agree to something before the young man retreated to the oak door that led to the auction room.

"Who was that?"

"Someone wants make us deal for doll. We have meeting now?"

I looked to the podium. The girl who'd welcomed us was tidying it and setting out water glasses for the auctioneer.

"Can't it wait? Why now?"

"Someone wants to make deal before auction. *Pashli!*"

I rose and Charlotte followed me. The three of us edged our way out towards the door. The navy-suited man who'd spoken to Nadyezha opened the door with an ingratiating grin, then led us in to a side room where someone about my age sat at a huge polished desk. Behind him stood a giant with a face like boiled beetroot and an overly muscular body that had run to fat, packed inside a silk suit like supermarket steak in clingfilm.

"Aha! Thomas and Charlotte – and Nadyezha! Thank you for joining me. I am Louis Grazinsky. Perhaps you know word of me?"

One never likes to offend someone who thinks you must know of them. But I didn't know him, and one look at Charlotte told me she didn't either. Nadyezha, however, spared us our blushes:

"Owner Tomsk Football Club, Siberia. True businessman modern Russia," she gushed.

Grazinsky grinned and leaned forward, selecting a thin Romeo y Julieta cigar from a *humidor* on his desk. He rolled the cigar between his fingers then perched it in his left hand. Beetroot-head reached forward and clipped one end off the cigar. Grazinsky put it in his mouth, then Beetroot whipped out a lighter and lit his boss's smoke.

Grazinsky puffed hard a few times, then spoke without removing the cigar from his mouth:

"We have no time before auction. I man of action. If do auction, is possible get $10,000,000." He paused, looking for any reaction. Much as I'd love to tell you I kept my poker face, in truth I was too stunned to react. What was this Slavonic *Yakuza* going to propose?

"However, is also possible get 2,000,000. Or nothing, if fail reach reserve. On other hand, I make you deal. $6,000,000 for Russian doll. Right now."

"But how do we know you'll pay up?"

Grazinsky removed the cigar from his mouth. He exhaled a thin stream of smoke.

"Is simple."

He clicked his fingers and nodded at Beetroot-head, who reached below the desk and pulled up a hard-shell briefcase. Once opened, it revealed thick wads of thousand-dollar US bills. "$6,000,000," Grazinsky said. "Cash."

Then he looked at me. "And I like man who makes up mind," he added.

Charlotte nodded quickly at me. Nadyezha put her hand on my arm.

"*Eto* 'all cash', *e tak li?*" she queried.

Grazinsky smiled. "Yes, madame. All cash. Right now."

I told him we'd take it and asked him to get the auction stopped. That left the problem of how to get $6,000,000 in cash out of Russia with no one noticing. Grazinsky left the room with his assistant to stop the sale, Nadyezha following him. As I struggled to get the briefcase off the desk, she passed me and whispered:

"About exit cash from Russia. Not worry. I know someone who work magics for us."

§

We took the money from Louis Grazinsky and returned to the Baltshug. On entering our suite, we agreed to take $150,000 each to cover immediate expenses. Charlotte made a donation of $10,000 to the Royal Society for the Protection of Cruelty to Animals, then announced her intention to purchase a small place in the Cotswolds. To that end she began flicking through the property pages in copies of *The Lady* and *Country Life* which she'd brought from England.

For my part, I was glad just to pay off my overdraft and credit card, arrears I'd built up in anticipation of Granny's estate. I kept $5,000 back so I could give Judy and David, my kids, a little surprise as well. Maybe then they'd speak to their feckless father more than twice a year.

Nadyezha snatched her $150,000 cash, threw it on her bed and rolled around, alternately purring and laughing.

"Ah, Peter. My Pete. If only you still on live. But I spend for you, darling. Not worry."

Our revels aside, *tempus fugit*, as the Latins taught us: and after a bottle of vintage Krug and two ounces of caviar *malossol*, the problem of how to get five and a half million US dollars out of Russia and into the UK remained.

§

"Anton Golodnya is good man," said Nadyezha as we barrelled down Ulitsa Vavarka to meet Golodnya the next morning, rather too close to Red Square for my liking. We bowled along not in a Lada that stank of micturate, but in a brand-new Mercedes S600 with blacked-out windows. "He will regulate problem, you see."

In fact, regulation of any kind, especially financial, was what we sought to ignore. After welcoming us to his office, located rather too close to the Kremlin for my liking, Anton Golodnya lit a fresh cigarette off the dog-end of his last one and gave us his terms from behind a cheap Formica desk.

"I buy tins of sprats and gherkins with money. Export England. Australia. Wherever is Russian. I sell sprats and gherkins. On sale, I return your money. Guaranteed. My term is ten per cent of principal. No negotiable."

The company literature in Golodnya's antechamber proclaimed him one of Russia's leading canned and bottled goods exporters. Enormously fat and sweating constantly, he chain-smoked tarry Carpathian cigarettes and brushed strands of brilliantined hair away from his eyes every few minutes.

Golodnya grew his hair long to cover a bald patch the size of Lake Baikonur. Such vanity can be useful, especially in a business partner one wishes to exploit for shady purposes. But ten per cent was a lot: more than half a million dollars for selling a few canned fish and vegetables. Or laundering our money, depending on how you saw it.

"Mr Golodnya, you have our agreement."

I offered my hand for a shake. He struggled to his feet and took my hand between both of his, shaking it warmly. Then he inclined his head in Charlotte's direction, offering his hand. When she took it he bent further, a struggle given his massive girth, and kissed her fingertips gently.

"*Otchen kharascho*," Golodnya said. "Everything will be fine."

Charlotte shot me a disbelieving look as we left Golodnya's office.

"I can't believe you just gave a man more than half a million dollars for exporting dead fish and pickles," she said in the Merc as we sped back to the hotel, her copy of *Country Life* folded to the property page which she'd marked with the printed receipt from her charitable donation.

"Fear not," I responded, then pointed to the copy of *Country Life*. "Now, are you leaning more towards Wiltshire's rolling hills, or perhaps an Oxfordshire bolthole?"

§

The next day, Charlotte wanted to buy some trinkets. Well, more than trinkets. Some vulgar pseudo-antiques she could show off to the well-heeled friends she'd soon have in the Cotswolds. All talk of saving pit ponies or whatnot abated as the money took hold. Nadyezha accompanied her to Dom, that most "new Russian" of department stores, while I packed my bags and enjoyed lunch at the hotel bar.

As I finished the final morsels of a sublime smoked trout salad, paired with an unostentatious half-bottle of white burgundy, my phone rang. Unidentified caller.

"Thomas?"

I affirmed my identity to my interlocutor.

"Louis Grazinsky. Doll fake. I want money back."

Blood shot up my neck and flushed my cheeks.

"What do you mean, a fake? That's impossible. It was validated by two experts."

Grazinsky chuckled.

"Not sure about England. But here, experts do anything for money. Is fake. Trust me."

I looked about me. No panicking, Tommy boy.

"Well, give the bally thing back to me then!"

"Not so simple – I already donate to Yekaterinburg Museum. Is useless anyway."

"Why should I give you the money if I can't get my doll back?"

Grazinsky snorted incredulously.

"Why? Why? Because Misha – man from yesterday, fat, suit, red face? Misha bring you hell on earth. This is why. I come Baltschug now and show you. Five minutes."

§

Ten minutes later I stood in our suite with Louis Grazinsky and Mr Beetroot, aka Misha. Misha / Beetroot stood too close to me for my comfort, arms folded across his overdeveloped chest.

As I saw it, I had three choices: argue with them, which would almost certainly result in my demise; steal my allegedly fake doll from this alleged museum in Yekaterinburg, or give them back their money. I took the better part of valour, or cowardice, and decided to return the money. The only problem was that I didn't have it – we'd given Anton Golodnya the lot yesterday.

"We have already invested our money, Mr Grazinsky. I mean, your money. You know what I mean."

Misha the Beetroot pushed his face into mine. Then he opened his jacket to reveal a knuckle-duster and some other instrument of torture, though I am no specialist in such matters. I swallowed hard.

"That said, I do believe I may be able to retrieve your money. I would need seventy-two hours to do so. And I must travel to England. Of course, your associate would be welcome to accompany me to assure the safe return of your funds."

I attempted a wan grin. Misha the Beetroot looked as if plucking my head from my shoulders like a grape would bring him sexual ecstasy. Mercifully, Grazinsky agreed to my plan.

That evening, the four of us – the two ladies, myself and Misha – found ourselves in the first class lounge at Sheremetyevo for the six p.m. flight to London. First class! And I was forced to splash out for Misha's ticket – though I had yet to tell Charlotte and Nadyezha that we had to hand back the money. I thought I'd save that for when we got back to England. Not twenty-four hours after I'd paid off my credit card, the bills had begun to mount once more. Would I ever be free from my own licentious spending?

The two ladies were away at Duty Free putting a dent in their share of the money while I swallowed Glenlivet like iced tea, trying to calm my nerves. As departure approached, Misha indicated the need to answer a call of nature, using his hands to mimic a giant phallus before his trousers and making a pissing sound. Then he rose, patted me on the back and vanished in the direction of the gentlemen's conveniences.

That he did not return to catch the flight was first a relief, then a concern; that Nadyezha had also vanished was simply a relief – although that relief was to be short-lived. When Charlotte returned empty-handed from the shops, I asked her what she'd been up to. She explained that she'd agreed to purchase a charming little cottage near Salisbury – a snip at a mere £750,000.

There was nothing for it. I would have to tell her Grazinsky wanted his money back. But I'd wait until we were airborne. She might be less strident then.

§

I shall spare you Charlotte's descriptions of me after I broke the news. Before telling her, I availed myself copiously of the Armagnac *fine* British Airways offers first-class passengers; after I told her, Charlotte drowned herself in vintage champagne until the glass was forcibly removed from her hand by cabin crew prior to landing. Then:

"Thomas, you are a contemptible fool" (a paean compared to her earlier harangues.) "By the way, Susan couldn't reach you, so she telephoned me before take-off to say your home is being repossessed unless you pay the mortgage arrears. And she's already told Judy and David they're going to be set for life. So good luck, you spineless oaf!"

On arriving at Terminal Five, I learned from my dear lady wife, the aforementioned Susan, that I had indeed received an eviction notice. I had no luck in trying to locate Nadyezha by phone or email, either. Charlotte refused to speak to me as she was too busy placating an estate agent in Wiltshire who threatened to sue her. Purse-lipped with anger, Susan had left our house and holed up in an expensive hotel, where my children were comforting her. But they were no longer speaking to me.

Meanwhile, I had the small matter of $6,000,000 owing to the Russian mafia. Notwithstanding such choppy waters, I sensed the worst was yet to come – and how right I was.

The next morning I received an unwelcome missive via motorcycle courier. The courier did not dismount, speak or remove his helmet. He merely held up an envelope at our garden gate and honked his horn until I appeared. As soon as I took the envelope, he shot off at high speed.

The one-page letter inside read:

Dear Thomas,

This difficult brief to writing. As I think possible you notice, Golodnya and I are been close and I will adopt him as second husband since Peter is buried.

Because of this and Golodnya leaving off his wife, I need all monies from sprats and gherkins. Mr Golodnya have several properties across world and is protectee from Russian mafia. Therefore my sincere advises is not to seek revenge on me.

I think bible saying correct: money tree-trunk of all evil. So I have took money to protect you from concupiscence of flesh.

Try be happy with what is.

Sincere your regards, Nadyezha

§

Never mind the condition of the bed-sitting room the local council found us until I arrange the sale of our few valuables. And let us ignore Susan's rage, my children's brooding silence (so much for my wished-for better times), and the ignominious notices from my bank and credit card company. All such pains will no doubt pale when Louis Grazhinsky comes to seek his revenge. I am more or less a dead man walking. However, I thought you might like to see a headline from the BBC this morning:

Ultra-Rare Russian Dolls by Faberge sell at auction for $20 million

PARIS — Thought to come from a private collection, one of the rarest pieces of pre-Revolutionary Russian art, long believed lost, has sold to a private collector for more than $20 million in a hotly-contested sale at Sotheby's in Paris....

Anti-social

Before this contract came through, Ken McKenzie's life was the same as it had always been: pretending to read Schopenhauer and Swedenborg, drinking tea and wondering when his money would run out.

Ken also loved scrolling through social media on his phone: lately, his self-image as a poet-philosopher vagabond had been eroded by his addiction to "SoMe," as hipsters call it.

It didn't matter who was posting, Ken loved social media almost as much as he loved being on disability benefits without being disabled. Take this tweet by Ken's pal Donald Crawford, part-time business communications tutor at some MBA factory in southwest England:

> Absolutely disgusted. Forty-seven years old, MSc in psychology, PhD in Creative Writing. No pension, no savings. I'd have been better as a plumber #nointellectualsallowed.

This was nonsense. Donald inherited his mother's holiday home in France twenty years ago. He'd also enjoyed a succession of pensionable interim lecturing jobs. His best move, though, was to impregnate a student from a wealthy family. Said family set the expectant couple up in a comfortable three-bedroom semi with a cleaner and all mod cons. Happy days – though you wouldn't know it from Don's Twitter feed.

§

Saturday afternoons would find Ken outside a pub, pint before him and cigarette in the ashtray as he pimped the pub's free WiFi while developing a fine case of tweeter's thumb. This post from Paul, an estate agent mate, made Ken want to pull out a metaphorical cat-o'-nine-tails:

Just sold to clients who couldn't be happier. Then steak and red wine with my darlings #bliss #family.

The truth? Paul dreamed of being a radio DJ and considered estate agency an affront to his talent. Paul's wife was about to leave him, she was so sick of him whining about his dreams.

Not long after he read that message, Ken finally cracked. It was a tweet from some folk band that set him off.

§

Weissweg, the band in question, played midweek gigs in pubs. You know: audiences applauding tune-ups, gnat's-piss beer and sour white wine. But their breathless tweeting suggested they thought they were Beyoncé:

> Delighted to announce our first-ever #nationaltour in support of our #newsingle, The Wyld Rose Is Sown. weisswegtheband. com

Their website revealed this "national tour" consisted of three local pubs that hosted the aforementioned midweek amateur nights. Ken piled in:

> @Weisswegtheband no' bad mate. Three local boozers. Is @Coldplay or @CalvinHarrisofficial supporting? See ya doon the dole!X

Weissweg banned him. But being banned just encouraged Ken to greater things.

§

After he'd been banned by the band, as it were, Ken began bursting bubbles in earnest. The more he trashed people, the worse (or better) things got. His follower numbers rose – modestly at first, from 48 bots and trolls to a whopping 247 curated, winnowed-out followers.

He started with an easy target: politicians. However, bubble-bursting them was an overcrowded market – easy meat, and everyone was at it. Newspaper comment sections also proved good sport since they were echo chambers for students, the terminally angry and the retired / bored. But Ken wanted juicier prey. People who might actually care if he exposed their vanity.

He didn't have to look far: middle-managers boasting of fake he-man exploits on the weekends; stressed female executives asserting earth-mother status via photos of cranberry-apricot muffins; has-been sportsmen claiming fellowship with today's stars. He went after the lot and spared none.

For all he got blocked, he picked up more followers. His 247 followers soon swelled to 3,223. A week later, he was up to 6,391 thanks to a few more spats.

§

A month later Ken was measuring his followers in the high five figures, his numbers popping like a firecracker on coke. Then he got that phone call.

Ken feared it was the police looking to investigate a benefits scam that ended a year ago when the presumed-dead target of his identity-theft operation was proven to still walk among us. But it wasn't the police. Instead it was one Ayesha Kirschbaum, who said she worked for the "Social Media Alliance" in California.

She had a proposal for Ken – and wanted to "hop on a Zoom call" to discuss it.

§

The next day, Ken found himself outside his local before opening time. This last happened when he'd collapsed in their beer garden the summer before to be woken by the rising sun, stale beer on his tongue and a burned-out cigarette in his fingers.

He needed to steal the pub WiFi for his Zoom call. He booted up his ancient computer, a process that took so long Ken wanted to boot its pixelated arse. Minutes later, Ken found himself peering into a home office on the other side of the world.

A youngish woman with a dark ponytail stared out of his cracked laptop screen. She wore a red rollneck sweater and a chunky necklace. In the top right corner, he saw two equally youngish men sporting glasses, white shirts and dark pastel ties.

"Ken? Ken McKenzie?"

"Yup, 'tis I! Ayesha? What can I do you for?"

Ken wanted a smoke. But it took him four attempts to get his laptop lid to stay open before he could roll up.

"Ken? You still there?"

"Aye man! Still here," Ken shouted, hands deftly flicking together a rollie.

"Cool! OK, so I am Ayesha, and these are my colleagues Mike and Neil. We represent the Social Media Alliance—"

Ken smirked. "Are ye's calling to take me down?"

"Oh no, not at all!" Ayesha protested.

Ken looked across the pub garden, rich with discarded glasses and assorted rubbish. The morning sun struggled to cut through the chill Scottish air.

"My colleague Mike Nesbitt has a proposal to put to you. Over to you, Mike!"

Mike's image slid forward on the screen. Ken drew hard on his rollup, blowing smoke into Mike's preppy physiognomy from 7,000 miles away.

"Hey Ken! Good to meet you!"

Ken waved, smiling at the absurdity of speaking to a bunch of yuppies in sunny California from a nut-bustingly cold Scottish beer garden.

"Awright, big man?"

"So Ken, we've noticed your recent popularity on Twitter…."

"Aye mate. Popular like Pol Pot, eh? Just seein' how many fowk I can piss off at once, hen?"

Mike smiled a thin-lipped smile. "Ken, you may know a lot of social media platforms are struggling these days…."

"Struggling? I'm no' surprised, mate. Struggling how, but? Doon tae their last ten billion?"

Ken blew more smoke at the screen, then tossed his still-burning fag-end on the concrete. The sun crept over the chimney tops.

"Social media is in a battle for engagement. That means we need people to start posting more, following more, liking more."

"Right, mate. But it's all shite. That's why I'm trying to take people down, eh?"

"We know. But that's why you're popular. You're the UK's rising social media star and in the European top ten growers."

"Naw, mate, eh? Well, there you are. My ma'll be proud at last!"

Ken spluttered and a little spittle hit his screen. He reached for his tobacco pouch as the third figure slid into view. This guy looked like a carbon copy of Mike Nesbitt, only with more grey hair, a bright yellow tie and different glasses.

"Ken, this is Neil Lafferty. I'm legal counsel at the Social Media Foundation. We want to offer you a job."

"A job as what? Tormenter in chief?"

"More or less, yes. We are prepared to pay you a quarter of a million dollars a year, starting immediately, to continue abusing celebrities, politicians, journalists and the general public. Within the grounds of certain…legal constraints, of course."

"Constraints? Like no slander or libel, that sort of thing?"

Neil Lafferty nodded. Mike Nesbitt chimed in.

"Essentially, we want to pay you for being you. Just keep doing what you're doing."

Now it was Ayesha's turn to pile on the charm. She drew a little closer to her camera and Ken noticed her perfect teeth.

"It's money for nothing, Ken!"

"Is it now?" Ken readied his next cigarette. He sparked up with his Space Alien Zippo. "I'm a philosopher to trade. And I'll tell ye this: there's no such thing as money for nothing. No' unless you're me. See, I've already got funds."

Ken chose not to tell them said funds came from his fake disabled status. Alongside a bit of casual glass-collecting in pubs if he was short that week.

"We're prepared to negotiate," Ayesha countered. "What's essential is that you understand what you bring to the table. We want your capacity to re-excite people in social media. That's what our advertisers are jonesing for."

She paused, looking to her left as if her colleagues were with her, not sat in spare bedrooms across San Francisco like battery hens blinking and wobbling after laying an egg.

"Look Ken, let's cut the bullshit. People are getting tired of social and we need to get them back. Who knew, but you're making it happen. Don't see this as a job. Just see it as encouragement, that's all."

"Hmmmm…." Ken sipped his coffee. "I'll need to speak to my agent."

"You have an agent?"

"Naw. But it felt good saying that."

The three talking heads laughed in that hollow way some people do. Ken sipped his coffee.

"Listen, boys and girls. You get me that contract and I'll think about it, awright?"

"Sounds good, Ken. Give me your email and I'll send it right away. If you decide to join us, please print and sign."

"Sweet. But I cannae afford the post tae America, I'll tell you that for free."

They told Ken it was no problem: all expenses would be paid. A courier would come and pick up the contract when he was ready.

§

That's how Ken found himself with a contract in front of him in his council flat, the figure of $250,000, plus a signing bonus of $10,000, burning a hole in his mind. Would he sign? Not to do so would be insanity. Riches and salvation, just for being himself.

And yet his models, his masters, all those philosophers whose works he opened and pretended to read, would not have approved. Bowing before the corporate beast.

Ken decided he'd have a smoke and think about it. He rolled up and stuck the fag in his mouth. Then he fished out his lighter and flicked at it. The flame flashed up from his Space Alien Zippo, the familiar smell of sparking flint and kerosene filling the air in his tiny kitchen.

He looked down at the contract and around himself at the cramped confines of his flat, the traces of damp on the walls. The couple next door started another row, so loud the football calendar hung precariously on the wall above his kitchen table started shaking.

He picked up the contract with his free hand, the burning lighter in the other. Then he lit his cigarette. As he inhaled his first draw, he slowly moved the pages of the contract toward the lighter's bright yellow flame….

Resignation

To Harry Furniss, working for a corporation felt like wearing a clown suit: a façade that made it easy to avoid taking anything seriously. After all, working for a global brand lubricates some people's social lives better than a bottle of Scotch. Turn up at some hotel bar, and before long a slightly heavy nonentity in middle-manager casuals (polo shirt, belted chinos worn above the navel) will ask what business you're in. After comparing your burdens, from regulation to office politics, you'll stagger back to your room with a card in your pocket, plus an invitation to visit him and his wife next time you're in Pensacola. Or Reykjavík. Or wherever.

Today, Harry has that clown suit on. He's meeting one of his company's senior vice presidents, or SVPs. Someone who has flown all the way from the Big Apple to Runcorn, Cheshire, to meet exclusively with Harry – and sixty-eight other members of the field support team at Starfish Technologies.

According to his LinkedIn profile, this SVP is "Global Head of Compliance, Financial Controls Unit" – what used to be called a regulatory manager. That long job title suggests a level of personal aggrandisement it would be foolish to dismiss when weighing up the man's character. His corporate headshot, much Googled since the announcement of his visit last week, shows a man in early middle age, balding, a slight smile about his lips. The photo hints at his belief there could be no greater adventure than to manage regulatory compliance at a manufacturer of radio gizmos.

Harry held his security pass up to the bleeper on the second floor like an animal being herded towards ritual sacrifice. The bleeper bleeped its satisfaction, and Harry walked through into a maze of glass cubicles – designed either to foster a spirit of collaboration and openness, or (as was equally likely) to stop people from pimping the free WiFi in the office. Yes, in this age when anyone can access any information from anywhere at any time, good old curtain-twitching, paranoiac snooping is making a raging comeback. Only it's virtual and digital now, so we can pretend it's not happening. Sort of.

Harry slung his black leather bag on a hot desk in the middle of the room and nodded to a colleague who had drowned herself in music, headphones on as she tapped away at her keyboard. He sat down, placing his cardboard coffee cup of coffee on the fake wooden Formica hot desk. Harry couldn't remember when it had become OK to listen to music while working, but it definitely was OK these days.

The quiet of concentration punctuated by low discussion had been replaced by music's hiss and swish and the clack of keyboards, big fat ghetto headphones clamped on people's domes like stun guns in an abattoir. Knocking, they called the practice: when you place the electrodes at the cow's temples and – ZAP – they feel nothing afterwards.

"Ready for the arrival of *le grand fromage*, are we, Harry?"

Harry looked up. The speaker was Jimmy Currey, office prankster and friend: someone who would never be seen dead wearing headphones in the office. A working-class lad from the Wirral who'd been educated into a world his family couldn't understand, Jimmy had a double PhD in physics and electronic engineering that had taken him away from a life of driving buses or labouring. Yet he'd retained a good working-class honesty and sense of humour, neither of which were especially useful at Starfish Technologies.

Jimmy's tie hung at half-mast under his collar. The sides of the collar stubbornly refused to meet in the middle; his grey-white hair, three months adrift from its last cut, bushed wildly from his shiny pate. Whenever the higher-ups called for a town-hall meeting, Jimmy could be seen ringing an imaginary bell and shouting "Oyez! Oyez! More corporate ballocks fresh from the bull's arse! Come and get it! More spin than a tumble dryer, right this way!"

This performance, together with other stunts including the exposure of his manhood while turning out his pockets to mimic an elephant, swearing at his boss while hiding under a desk and making false confessions of alcoholism in client meetings, had hardly marked him out for superstardom. In fact, at the age of fifty-three, it was a safe bet that Jimmy Currey couldn't wait either to retire or get fired. And preferably the latter, with a fat pay-off that would enable the former.

Harry felt blessed to know someone who had long breathed deep of corporate life's steaming dunghill, yet still swallowed every last morsel of shit he was given. And that without a word of complaint. At least not to the management. Too old and uninterested to harbour any ambition, yet too young to retire; not poor enough to suffer, but not rich enough to stop working – that was Harry. And Jimmy. And millions of others.

"My knees are trembling in anticipation," Harry replied in answer to Jimmy's non-question. Harry opened his laptop and fired up his email.

"I know you'd like them knees to tremble in rhythm with Pippa's, but that's not on the menu, chum," Jimmy replied, popping a piece of nicotine gum in his mouth – yet another futile attempt to quit smoking.

Ah, Pippa. Pippa McMahon. Starfish Technologies' UK SVP. That type of woman teenage boys fantasise about – before they grow up and learn to avoid her like Ebola, open sewers or parking violations in major cities. Pippa McMahon was the head of Starfish Technologies' Manchester "hub" – office to you and me. At forty-three, she was single, teetotal, rich, gluten-intolerant, obsessed with reality TV and endowed with a personality that could put the devil in a headlock.

The term "cow," now largely a cliché and far too cursory to do her various forms of spiritual ugliness justice, was insufficient; Harry found himself reaching for phrases from the Revelation to St John the Divine whenever he thought about her. In Harry's febrile imagination, he would imagine Pippa dicing on her carpet with centurions, using human souls as gambling chips during her monthly "Town Hall Update"; her "management by walking around" became visitations of the noonday devil, and even her number flashing on Harry's desk phone became, in his mind, an algorithm of the number of the beast.

Pippa was so self-absorbed she worked out religiously for ninety minutes a day, got her hair and nails done weekly and was, as Jimmy would put it with tongue adrift and eyebrows semaphoring lust, "a presentable lass". And no doubt she would be sat next to the guy coming today – she sat next to all the important visitors.

Harry pictured her twiddling her necklace, smiling at this guy every five seconds, laughing at his jokes and flicking her hair. Just as surely, the assembled staff would be staring out the window, sipping coffee or looking at the presentation on the wall – anything to avoid witnessing the flirtatious Rabelaisian festival visited by Pippa of Babylon on Starfish Technologies' Compliance Weenie.

Then Harry heard his email ping:

REMINDER: Staff Town Hall meeting with Rob McMillan, 10AM. Edison Room.

Rob McMillan, SVP and Global Head of Compliance, FCU, will present a corporate update today in the Edison Room at 10AM. Attendance at this meeting is mandatory for all STM (Starfish Technologies Manchester) employees.

Thank you –

Pippa

Pippa McMahon

Senior Vice President and Office Lead

Starfish Technologies Manchester

Starfish: Enabling the New Golden Age of Wireless

"That it then, mate? Off to open our mouths beneath the next arse-dump from some teenage bigwig?" Jimmy asked, looking over Harry's shoulder at the missive from Pippa-who-must-be-obeyed, passive-aggressive sign-off and all. Never have the two words "thank you" been imbued with more veiled malice than when used at the end of a Pippa McMahon email. Jimmy scratched his chin while staring at Harry's screen, then:

"Here, I'm dying for a fag, me. Do you think we've got time—"

But Pippa's secretary's voice boomed over the PA: "Attention all employees. Please make your way to the Edison Room, where Rob McMillan will be presenting at ten a.m. Please note attendance at this meeting is mandatory."

"Fooks' sake, this must be an important one," Jimmy opined. "I thought he were only the regulatory manager. Wonder why they've sent him? Are we getting a bonus? Is Runcorn the next Silicon Valley or summat?"

Harry drained his coffee and tossed the paper cup at his bin. It bounced off the rim, teetered then went in.

"Bingo, mate," said Harry. "Only by the time Runcorn becomes Palo Alto, you and me will be either retired or dead."

Harry was ten years younger than Jimmy. Despite the age gap, he was if anything even more stained and pickled, more steeped in cynicism about corporate life. For Harry, the number of people employed to do non-jobs (including himself) at Starfish suggested they must be overcharging customers to afford all these hangers-on. Harry stood up, creases in his tired suit, dress shoes more scuffed than they should be, and motioned towards the corridor behind Jimmy's sloping shoulders:

"For God and England, Jimmy?"

"Cry Harry, for God and St George!" answered Jimmy. And with that, our two middle-aged nonentities sallied forth unto the field of corporate endeavour.

§

There was a good crowd in the Edison Room, though nothing like the crowd there should have been for an SVP from New York. But a forty-five-minute meeting with the global head of Compliance hardly sets hearts aflutter; most of the salesmen had booked client meetings to avoid this presentation, while other staff discovered urgent medical appointments they couldn't get out of, meetings with head teachers, or something else to skip this. But how wrong they were to have missed it, how wrong.

Rob McMillan fulfilled the promise of his corporate headshot. A man on the fringes of middle-age, ruddy of cheek and unapologetically balding, sporting a neat charcoal suit without a tie and those light brown leather buckled brogues that always betray deep pockets and little dress sense.

He sat at the middle of the head table in the Edison Room, Pippa McMahon at his side, a thick gold chain around her neck with some type of higher-rent fashion branding on it. Her black pant suit was nipped in at the waist and she wore an expensive-looking T-shirt, her hair pulled back in a girlish ponytail.

Harry sat next to Jimmy as the room filled up, Pippa's giggles and titters reaching them like the cries of some spliced-gene miscegenate as she succumbed mentally to Rob McMillan's testosterone-fuelled banter. He was the thick-muscled God of Compliance, she the supplicant nymph. Harry stared blankly ahead. Seconds passed, then Jimmy leaned in at his side:

"What she's really trying to tell him is she'd let him, you know," Jimmy muttered, his breath all mint nicotine gum and tobacco.

"Either that, or she wants to tune his flesh transceiver," Harry offered.

There was enough of a crowd now, and time was a-wasting. Pippa stood up and raised her hands for silence. On the wall behind her, the Starfish Technologies logo glowed large in a PowerPoint slide: a brown (unfortunate choice of colour) version of the eponymous submarine echinoderm with the words "STARFISH TECHNOLOGIES" in blue next to it and the strapline, "Enabling the New Golden Age of Wireless" underneath.

"Thank you for coming to this important meeting about our future at Starfish Technologies. Rob McMillan, global head of Compliance, has some news for you. So, without further ado – Rob?"

McMillan stood, thanked Pippa, then cleared his throat.

"Good morning, team," he said, one or two scamps at the back muttering "good morning" back, much like rollcall back in primary school. McMillan's voice sounded vaguely English, vaguely educated, with some American inflections. No doubt he'd joined Starfish straight out of uni, then been "seconded" to the US. His was a world of strategies and charts, not one of doing the bare minimum for eight hours then bunking off to get home in time for the kids.

"I have some important news," McMillan said, a slight stammer infecting his voice, the colour in his cheeks rising.

Realisation hit Harry like the garden wall hits your car when you're reversing up the driveway. Of course – fearless corporate warriors that they were, the board had dispatched a junior to let us have it. The weenie cometh, wielding an axe.

"As some of you will know, the last two quarters haven't been great for the company and its investors," McMillan began.

Harry heard the strains of Terence Trent D'Arby's "If You Let Me Stay" in his head. He half-expected McMillan to break into song, begging his listeners to put their bags down, okay? Cos he definitely doesn't want us to leave. If we let him staaaaa-aayyyayyyy…. Instead, McMillan flicked at his laptop and a chart with spidery lines appeared. Harry was no expert, but it looked like a screen grab from a financial terminal. Next to him, Jimmy muttered, "Bugger me, that's crap."

At least Jimmy knew what it meant. Harry would have to ask him later. McMillan looked up at his silent if not rapt audience, then down again at his script. He proceeded to read laboriously, his cheeks reddening all the while.

"Our stock has underperformed both at an alpha level – its absolute performance – and at beta, against market. Orders are down, and projected sales are poor. Which means the marketplace expects us to take action."

Harry wondered idly why bigwigs always said "the marketplace," a phrase that invited images of kindly old women and cobbled squares in southern Europe, rather than sharp-suited guys with soft hands who owned yachts, private islands and watches studded with jewels.

"We will implement a workforce management programme, or WFM. As part of the WFM for Q3, we have identified a number of key roles in Starfish Technologies Manchester that will be secured."

McMillan looked up. He had the audience's attention now, all right. Jimmy was the only one not looking at McMillan or the screen; he'd probably heard this a million times before. Jimmy whispered "BUT" at Harry, then winked. "There's always a but…."

"However," McMillan continued, his balding scalp now glowing with perspiration, "a further segment will be eligible for our voluntary redundancy programme, or VRP. Those who wish to apply for VRP may do so via their local office manager—" and here, McMillan looked up and glanced at Pippa McMahon, who smiled encouragingly. "There will be preferential terms for those over fifty years of age."

Jimmy made a fist-pumping motion and whispered "Yeeeeeess!"

At the front of the room, McMillan took a sip of water from the bottle on the lectern in front of him and sighed audibly. Poor little bastard, Harry reflected. He wasn't liking this any more than we were. Harry thought about the compensation figures from last year's annual report. Apparently, the chief financial officer made $15,000,000. Rumour had it he'd just bought an island in the Turks and Caicos. And now his stooge was here to tell everyone they were getting fired.

"Before I hand back to Pippa, I should say that if we do not achieve our headcount reduction target, there'll be at least one round of compulsory redundancies. As we are aiming to make a seventy per cent reduction in field sales and service staff from this location, I must advise you this is highly probable."

McMillan looked visibly relieved. "Right, that's the news. I'm sorry it's not better and I know how disappointing this will be. Now I'm happy to take any questions."

There was a moment's silence, then the hands rose: slowly at first, hesitantly, like flowers in early spring. Jimmy was one of those who put his hand up.

"Yes sir," McMillan said, pointing at Jimmy. Pippa McMahon's secretary walked towards Jimmy with a hand-held microphone, but Jimmy waved it away. On the podium, Pippa McMahon began twisting her hair faster, face frozen in a faint smile.

"Er…thank you. Can you hear me OK?," Jimmy asked, mock-cupping his hands in McMillan's direction. McMillan smiled and nodded, not fifteen feet away from Jimmy's seat in the middle of the audience. "Good," said Jimmy. "So basically, you are looking at taking us from an office of around seventy down to fifteen, is that it?"

McMillan nodded.

"Well, it's not all bad, is it? At least everyone's going to have their own private toilet, aren't they? Never mind "Find a Place Where You Can Shine" – you should change the recruitment poster to "Find a Place Where You Can Shite!"

The audience laughed. Jimmy stood up and gave a mock bow to his colleagues. A thin ripple of applause wreathed through the room and he sat again as the noise died down. "Seriously, though, mate –

you are going to close this office, aren't you? We're going to relocate, aren't we?"

Pippa McMahon leaned in to her microphone, smoothing away an imaginary crumb on her suit as she did so.

"Er, thank you for that contribution, Dr Currey. At this time, we've no information on whether or not a relocation is planned."

"Oh aye yeah, well right," muttered Jimmy to no one in particular. "They're closing us down, you mark my words."

§

When Harry came into work three weeks later, the atmosphere at Starfish Technologies was void. Void of people, of life, of purpose. No one hid the fact they were bunking off early: there was no need to schedule a client visit near your home so you could be outside the school gate at 3.30; no need to pretend the calls from recruitment consultants were really from friends. Instead, Harry found an emptiness in the office that would have made the *Mary Celeste* look like a pumping nightclub in the early hours of a bank holiday weekend.

After pretending to work for a few minutes, he went for a stroll and ran into Jimmy having a smoke outside the deliveries area at the back. Jimmy's rugby shirt had been washed too many times, its green and red stripes faded into incongruity, fabric tight over his impressive belly. He sucked greedily at a cigarette and raised his eyebrows as Harry approached.

"Now then our Harry," said Jimmy. "Are you one of the lucky ones then?"

"What do you mean?"

"I mean voluntary redundancy mate. Yours truly has been given the nod. That's fifteen years' service at two and a half weeks a year plus three months' notice and eighteen months' extra pension." Jimmy sucked hard at the butt of his cigarette then ground it out under his heel. "First thirty-five grand tax free. I am made up, fooking delighted, over the moon – all that. Three months off to let them see their mistake, then I'll come back and make double me current wage as a consultant, three days a week. Now what about you?"

"No idea. I've not heard a word. We'll have to see."

Jimmy sucked air through his teeth and smiled. "We'll see all right. I suspect you're going to be protected – only cos every man and his dog has applied for redundancy."

When Harry returned to his computer, he found a meeting request from Pippa McMahon in his inbox. Only the meeting wasn't in her office: it was in a coffee room on the ground floor, a room no one had used for years – not since the last lot got sacked a few years ago.

Twenty minutes later, Harry found himself facing Pippa McMahon and a lady in late middle-age across the drab meeting room. The lady was somewhat crumpled of hair and face, her appearance suggesting someone who had seen a lot of people cry. She wore a suit of pastel grey, lots of chunky jewellery and too much makeup. Pippa McMahon smiled ingratiatingly as Harry entered the room.

"Harry. Thank you for coming. As you can imagine, we have a lot of people to see today. This is Deborah Abrahams, our head of Human Resources. Harry, we have always valued your contribution to our company and I want to make sure we are honest with you."

Here we go, thought Harry.

"As you may know, we have received numerous applications for voluntary redundancy, and yours is one we will not be accepting. Given other planned changes, we have decided to ringfence your role. That means the only way for you to leave Starfish Technologies is to resign if you choose. The good news is that your job is safe, and you will not be selected for redundancy as part of our workforce management programme. Do you have any questions for Deborah or myself?"

Harry shook his head. As Pippa's rouged lips moved, he was vouchsafed a vision of the next fifteen to twenty years of his life: some faceless serviced office somewhere off the M6 motorway, the Starfish Technologies logo from here transported there to save money, its sharp edges squatting incongruously like a Styrofoam toad in some tiny shared reception area. The proverbial death by a million cuts "to help us realise investor expectations" before Harry, too, was pensioned off at some unspecified point to rake leaves, ponder package holidays and slowly develop some as yet unspecified and ultimately fatal age-related condition.

Deborah Abrahams' crumpled face unfolded to a grin. "It's good news for you, Harry. You're safe. We should tell you that at this time consultations are ongoing with the other fourteen members of staff who will be retained." Abrahams glanced at her wristwatch, then continued: "In about ten minutes, those subject to compulsory redundancy are going to be summoned to a meeting. If you wish, you may leave and return to work after lunch. We expect this news to be distressing for them."

Harry looked through the window to the slate roofs of the neighbourhood and the sky beyond, a dull tableau punctuated by thin patches of sunlight. Safe. Safe to keep working and earning a wage. As if being safe were all that mattered.

"Harry? Do you want to go home for a bit? Are you all right?"

Harry kept quiet. He was supposed to be happy about this. After all, he got to keep his job. But instead of relief, all he felt was numbness. More of the same. A slow decline, like when your legs got stuck to a metal slide in the playground when you were a kid. Not going anywhere. Stasis. Harry stood up, pushing his chair away from the table, and shook his head.

"Thank you, Harry!" Pippa sing-songed. "We're all looking forward to working with you, all right?"

Harry said his goodbyes, then walked out to his car and sat in it. Then he turned the ignition and listened to the engine. After a while he must have dozed off, the music on the radio fading to white noise as he drifted in and out of consciousness and the clouds overhead kept rolling by in an endless pattern whose meaning would remain a mystery to those of us existing on the earth below.

You Look Like You're Writing A Novel

They'd been developing these algorithms for decades. The old "You look like you're writing a letter" expanded to include, "You look like you're writing a poem," or similar. For any form you could think of, your computer provided suggestions: better grammar, corrections, emendations.

The writer started tapping:

Julia O'Brien put down her coffee and gazed at her mobile phone in disgust. What was meant to be a convenience had become an instrument of slavery. Her every utterance stored to be used against her by anyone with access, from brain-dead marketers to the intelligence services. Nominally free, in fact she was chained to an invisible, all-devouring algorithm.

The writer paused. Patches of his screen populated with dialogue boxes offering hints. These machines were so powerful now they had, if not minds of their own, then binary memories so enormous they operated like minds.

Julia imagined herself swimming, playing with childhood friends among kelp on the beach. Adulthood was worse today than it had been for centuries, since humanity was denied freedom of expression, everything monitored over the internet.

Then a dialogue box popped up: "You look like you're writing about the role of technology in society."

"No shit, Hal," the writer muttered. He clicked in the corner of the pop-up to remove the message. He placed his fingers on the keys.

Another dialogue box: "Are you aware that other writers such as Dick, Philip K., and Le Guin, Ursula K., have already tackled this theme?"

"Yes, I am!" the writer shouted, slapping his mouse down on the trackpad.

Just as he was about to type, another dialogue: "Risk of repetition is estimated at 93.7%. Do you really want to explore the same theme as other writers of greater ability? Other themes are available. Click here to read more."

"Greater ability? I'll give you—" he stopped himself in disgust. He stood up, chair falling back behind him. Time for a coffee: he headed for the kitchen.

§

It started forty years ago with the first spell checkers. Around the same time as people started paying to have their work considered by magazines. Back then, debate centred on the legitimacy of self-publishing, the ethics of paying to submit. Then came the grammar and style checkers. Writers became enveloped in a techno-cocoon, then redundant as conformity to moral and social norms came to matter more than truth, beauty or anything else.

The writer remembered when all he had was a notebook filled with furious scrawl skittering across pages like demented spiders. Pencil tips cracking, pen nibs bending under his raging fingers, the connection between hand and brain rapid, vital.

In the kitchen, he pressed a button on the espresso machine and watched as it gurgled and blew, doing things to beans he did not understand. As the coffee ran into his cup, the writer wondered how to get round his computer's trickery. Even without a connection, dialogue boxes advised you splatterpunk and cybercore were most likely to attract readers, that literary work would not sell, and that self-publishing was a great idea. Then the software tried to sell you stuff.

The writer drank his coffee, listening to Mozart's *Requiem* played by an Austrian orchestra over the internet. As he sipped, he reflected that someone, somewhere had recorded his love of Mozart. That person, or bot, had noted him listening to his internet radio during working hours.

The writer put down his cup and snorted. Even Mozart used technical assistance in the shape of his amanuensis, Franz Xaver Süssmayr, who completed the last four sections of the work after the maestro's demise. And if Mozart had lived now? He could have sketched some outlines and let an online composition tool do the rest. These days, Count von Walsegg-Stuppach would most likely have tried to write the *Requiem* himself. On a computer.

§

The writer finished his coffee and went back to the study. He sat down and stared at the words on the screen:

Julia O'Brien put down her coffee and gazed at her mobile phone in disbelief. What she'd seen as a torment was actually an instrument that enabled her to the point of omnipotence. Now she could record her every utterance and use it to fend off brain-dead marketers or even the secret intelligence services, as if they'd be interested in what she did or said. She was free, but willingly engaged with an invisible, all-enabling machine.

Then a dialogue box popped up: "You've self-identified this work as a novel. Are you sure it's not a political treatise? Please be aware of libel and slander legislation – false accusations of corporate malpractice may carry prison terms."

Shaking his head, the writer pressed a key to delete the message.

Then another dialogue box: "For your convenience, we have edited your text for style and grammar. Ready to upgrade? Go Pro with Wordly™: Shakespeare's power at a keystroke®!"

The strains of Süssmayr's Sanctus, one of his additions to the *Requiem*, floated into the study from the kitchen. Known to all as Mozart's work, this score was not his. These tones, this depth, this genius guaranteed Amadeus immortality – but he was cold in a pauper's grave when it was written. Today, computers acted as a cyber-Süssmayr for writers and – worse – as an instrument of control.

The writer shut his laptop and reached for his old notebooks. Still half full of fresh pages – enough to set down what had happened for some better, future time. He fished in his desk for his fountain pen and scratched at the page, watching the ink dry as the pen wrote, its meniscus fading like souring blood. And he no longer knew for whom he was writing, or why.

Acknowledgements

Thanks to the editors of the following publications in which these stories first appeared: *Murder, Ink* (Crimeucopia, UK, 2022), for "My Grandmother's Russian Doll"; *Samjoko* (South Korea), *Ars Notoria* (UK) and *Sterling Clack Clack* (USA) for "Crunch Time for the Pheasant".

"You Look Like You're Writing a Novel" won first prize in the Strands International Flash Fiction competition for November 2024. "For One Night Only" was the lead feature in *Makarelle* (UK) for Summer 2022, and was a finalist for the Wells Festival of Literature Award 2022 (UK). "Anti-social" was shortlisted for the Wells Festival of Literature Award 2021 (UK) and specially commended for the Bridgend Writers' Award 2022 (UK) before being published in *Ars Notoria* in early 2023.

"A Riveting Tale" first appeared in *God's Cruel Joke* in the USA, while "Resignation" was first published in *Idle Ink* (UK), and reprinted in *Workers Write!* (Worker's Council of America, 2024). "You Look Like You're Writing A Novel" first appeared in *Witcraft* (Australia) and *The Sprawl* (Canada). This story also won first prize in the Strands Short Fiction Competition (India) in November 2024.

Massive thanks to the *Ars Notoria* sodality for giving this wanderer a home, especially to Philip R. Hall and Paul Halas for creating *Ars Notoria* and AN Editions, and equally to Peter Cowlam, novelist and Literary Editor at *Ars Notoria*. Thank you to Pete Field for his inventive genius on the cover art. Finally, thanks to my family and friends, above all Tania, Rob and Andy. RIP DeeDee, 2019–24.

www.jwwoodwriter.net

Other Books and Authors at an Editions

*O*scar: *The Second Coming*, a graphic novel by Dan Pearce. When Oscar Wilde reappears in Reading Gaol exactly a century after his initial imprisonment in 1895, the event is greeted with disbelief, then denial – not least by Wilde himself.

Among prison staff and the judiciary, press and government, bewilderment turns to panic. With truly Wildean wit, Dan Pearce revels in a technology and attitudes much changed over a century or so, while people and their mores remain rooted in self-interest. In fact, those most willing to accept the regenerated Wilde on his own terms are his new cell mates, while the great and the good search in vain for political expedients, unable to face down the moral dilemma of a resurrected Oscar Wilde.

Pearce gives us a cavalcade of characters: the prison psychiatrist, the prison governor's wife, an art therapist, hardened and softened criminals, and more. Dan Pearce's facility with the medium of cartoon and his penchant for lampooning are reminiscent of Robert Crumb, Thomas Rowlandson and William Hogarth, though with an illustrative style purely his own.

It need not be stressed that continuity in the comics genre operates on a different basis from that of any other art form. To that end, with Pearce, complex and hyper-creative layouts are jettisoned in favour of straightforward storytelling, with a visual syntax unflaggingly hitting the mark.

'It's delightful! Very, very funny … Anyone with a true sense of him should find it wholly engaging!' **Stephen Fry**

The Rights of Man And Fish, a novel by Paul Halas. *The Rights of*

Man And Fish romps through more than 1,000 years of European history as seen through the eyes of a carp. An intelligent, acerbic, multi-lingual carp with a taste for Armagnac, patisserie and progressive politics. Gisella the carp is a one-off, and any resemblance to any other talking fish, either real or imagined, is not only incidental, but utterly impossible.

On her journey she meets such historical figures as William the Conqueror, Jane Austen, Alexander Pope and Pablo Picasso, as well as finding herself caught up in Da Vinci's experiments, various European wars, rows and love-affairs, not to mention a variety of alcohol-induced mishaps. Not only does she witness many of the great (and infamous) events of history, she is frequently the cause of them. Which is quite a feat for a fish with a brain the size of a walnut. She also overcomes the ongoing problem of how to talk to humans while remaining partially submerged, and avoiding barbs and hooks, both from anglers and philosophers.

Delightful, informative and sceptical – but never cynical – *The Rights of Man And Fish* nods to Voltaire, Günter Grass and Paul Torday's *Salmon Fishing in the Yemen*, while maintaining a humour and breadth of vision entirely its own. Join Gisella as she finds out what makes the ideal society based on what she learns from a millennium of human error, intrigue and haute cuisine.

That Was Hugo Blythe MP, a novel by Peter Cowlam. *That Was Hugo Blythe MP* is the professional journal, presented in diary form, of government researcher Alaric Casteele. Casteele's diary is a skilful interchange between events in his domestic life, and his meticulous eavesdropping into the political intrigues levelled against his boss Hugo Blythe, a government minister pivotal in the New Labour project, climaxing as a general election approaches. Casteele soon discovers the department he's been appointed to, and the ministers heading it, have enslaved themselves to the prevailing culture of celebrity, with its strictures of media visibility and attention to self-image. He further discovers that there are plots against his boss Hugo Blythe, and in gathering evidence to confirm his suspicions embarks on a strictly illegal means of surveillance, at great personal risk. His two principal suspects are the Right

Honourable Tamara Sorr MP, and the Right Honourable Arabella Jury MP – also of Hugo's department.